ON THE SPOT

*

'Killing a man seems pretty awful – in cold blood.'

Perelli shook his head.

'Killing a guy in hot blood – that's awful, because nine times in ten you make a mistake, and you kill somebody you wouldn't kill, that you didn't ought to kill. Look at the war, Jimmy – I was in that. Killing guys we didn't know – regular fellers, some of them. They'd done nothing wrong, but we just sailed in and killed them and they killed us. There's no sense to it. But when we bump off a man there's a reason, and when we do it it's been worth doing. The things you do in hot blood are generally foolish, and the things you do in cold blood are the worth-while ones.'

Also in Arrow Books by Edgar Wallace

Edgar Wallace

On the Spot

ARROW BOOKS

engaged as a correspondent to cover the South African War for Reuter and later for the *Daily Mail*. By an ingenious scheme he scooped the signing of the Peace Treaty. The *Daily Mail* was delighted; Lord Kitchener was furious and permanently banned him as a war reporter.

With the war at an end he became the first editor of the *Rand Daily Mail* but later returned to England to the London *Daily Mail*. Here as a reporter he covered crimes, trials and hangings. He stored up knowledge of crime and criminals and he learnt two practical lessons—economy of words and the ability to meet a deadline; and, later as racing correspondent for various papers, he acquired his affection for racing which proved invaluable for his books but highly detrimental to his bank balance.

His first novel *The Four Just Men* he published himself in 1905 but his success as an author stemmed from the stories of Africa which he wrote for the *Tale Teller* and which were later published as *Sanders of the River*.

During the years that followed he wrote books, plays and articles. His success and his enormous output—in 1926 he had 18 books published—enabled him to live in a far different way from the early days in Greenwich; but he was never ashamed of his early poverty but rightly proud of his achievement.

Edgar Wallace had a remarkable memory which enabled him to work out the complete plot of a new book without making notes; invariably he wrote the first page in longhand, dictating the rest to his secretary or into a dictaphone according to the time of day—for sometimes he would work far into the night and sometimes he would begin extremely early in the morning, always fortified by half-hourly cups of tea and with a plentiful supply of cigarettes to be smoked in his long holder. His powers of concentration were immense; his young children could go to his study at any time with their problems; sleepless guests would call in for a cup of tea—but these interruptions had no effect on his chain of thought.

He worked hard and almost his only relaxation was racing and, in the summer, a journey up the river to Maidenhead in his motor launch the *Miss Penelope*.

In November, 1931, Edgar Wallace took up yet another

Edgar Wallace

On the Spot

ARROW BOOKS

ARROW BOOKS LTD
3 Fitzroy Square, London W1

An imprint of the Hutchinson Group

London Melbourne Sydney Auckland
Wellington Johannesburg Cape Town
and agencies throughout the world

This revised edition first published by
John Long Ltd 1969
Arrow edition 1974

*Made and printed in Denmark
by A/S Uniprint*

ISBN 0 09 908410 4

Introduction

BY PENELOPE WALLACE

Whoever reads a book by Edgar Wallace has the feeling of knowing him, for he puts so much of himself into every page—his beliefs, his likes and dislikes and perhaps, above all, his sense of humour.

It was his contention that the writing of an author must be backed by experience and during his life he achieved experience in such varied fields as newsboy, printer, milkboy, medical orderly, publisher, special constable, war correspondent, journalist, racehorse owner, film director, playwright and author.

He was born in Greenwich on the 1st April, 1875. His father was an actor, his mother an actress—they were not married. When the boy was nine days old he was adopted by a Billingsgate fish porter and grew up in Greenwich and the surrounding parishes. Intelligent and observant, and having that quality of humanity which enabled him to understand as well as to observe, he acquired in his boyhood the knowledge and love of London and her people which can be felt in so many of his books.

After he left school he tried a variety of jobs ranging from printing to plastering. At eighteen he joined the Army. In 1896 his regiment was transferred to South Africa. Here he wrote a poem in honour of the arrival of Rudyard Kipling, *Good Morning Mr. Kipling*; he was hailed as 'The Soldier Poet' then in 1898 a book of his poems was published under the title *The Mission That Failed*. This was the first of the 173 books which were published in the following 34 years.

In 1899 he bought himself out of the Army and was

engaged as a correspondent to cover the South African War for Reuter and later for the *Daily Mail*. By an ingenious scheme he scooped the signing of the Peace Treaty. The *Daily Mail* was delighted; Lord Kitchener was furious and permanently banned him as a war reporter.

With the war at an end he became the first editor of the *Rand Daily Mail* but later returned to England to the London *Daily Mail*. Here as a reporter he covered crimes, trials and hangings. He stored up knowledge of crime and criminals and he learnt two practical lessons—economy of words and the ability to meet a deadline; and, later as racing correspondent for various papers, he acquired his affection for racing which proved invaluable for his books but highly detrimental to his bank balance.

His first novel *The Four Just Men* he published himself in 1905 but his success as an author stemmed from the stories of Africa which he wrote for the *Tale Teller* and which were later published as *Sanders of the River*.

During the years that followed he wrote books, plays and articles. His success and his enormous output—in 1926 he had 18 books published—enabled him to live in a far different way from the early days in Greenwich; but he was never ashamed of his early poverty but rightly proud of his achievement.

Edgar Wallace had a remarkable memory which enabled him to work out the complete plot of a new book without making notes; invariably he wrote the first page in longhand, dictating the rest to his secretary or into a dictaphone according to the time of day—for sometimes he would work far into the night and sometimes he would begin extremely early in the morning, always fortified by half-hourly cups of tea and with a plentiful supply of cigarettes to be smoked in his long holder. His powers of concentration were immense; his young children could go to his study at any time with their problems; sleepless guests would call in for a cup of tea—but these interruptions had no effect on his chain of thought.

He worked hard and almost his only relaxation was racing and, in the summer, a journey up the river to Maidenhead in his motor launch the *Miss Penelope*.

In November, 1931, Edgar Wallace took up yet another

profession, he went to Hollywood to write film scripts; he worked at his usual speed and in nine weeks he had written four scripts, including *King Kong*—this in addition to alterations to a play, short stories, articles and the long letters to his wife which were later published as *My Hollywood Diary*.

He planned that his family should join him in Hollywood before his return to England in April, 1932, but early in February he developed a sore throat; but this was no ordinary sore throat for rapidly it became double pneumonia and within three days he died. He died but his books have lived; fast moving and vital they have taken countless readers out of their ordinary lives and into the world of master criminals and little crooks; of murder and robbery. A world where right triumphs and a world which confirms that it is impossible not to be thrilled by Edgar Wallace.

On the Spot, first published in 1931, is set against the gangland life of Chicago during Prohibition.

The background is completely authentic and the characters—the Big Shots, their gunmen, their women—are faultlessly drawn not only as participators in the drama of that era but as believable and three-dimensional people.

Chicago 1929

1

Tony Perelli was not yellow, either by his own code or judged by standards more exacting. It was yellow to squeal to futile police, but not yellow to squeal to one's own crowd, and squeal loudly, about injustices suffered. It was yellow to betray a pal, but not yellow if the pal had not acted square or if he himself was yellow; even then it was yellow to tip off the police about his delinquencies. The honourable thing was to take him to some lone place and 'give him the works'.

Horrified farmers, who in the grey of morning found stark things sprawled on the edge of their lands, might grow hysterical about the brutality of it, but there it was; justice in a sense, the sort of justice that the west and the middle west understood and countenanced too frequently.

For instance, 'Red' Gallway.

Red had been most things that were wrong and done most things that were indictable. He had been peterman —which is a euphemism for safe-breaker—con man, hold-up man and keeper of questionable establishments. He came from this strenuous and not too affluent stew of professions into the business of booze running, which gave him wealth beyond his dreams, a comfortable existence, immunity from arrest, and the comradeship of square shooters. Success made him big in the head; he became talkative, a little quarrelsome; crowning offence, he began to sniff the white stuff.

Angelo Verona, the sleek chief of staff, expostulated.

'Say, Red, I'd cut out that stuff. Tony won't stand for coke in this outfit.'

9

Red's ugly face twisted in a sneer.

'Is that so?'

Angelo nodded, his grave, brown eyes on the weakling.

'Cocaine never did any good to anybody,' he said. 'Yeh! It makes you feel big for a while, but when the effect passes you're just a hole in the ground. And the first time they get a guy down at Headquarters to quiz him, why, he falls apart.'

'Is that so?'

'That—is—so,' nodded Angelo.

Red ran around with a friend—Mose Leeson, sometime machinest from Gary. The men had mean appetites in common, felt more at home in the squalor and dinginess of certain poor areas than in the splendour of lakeside restaurants.

To Leeson was due the credit of a discovery which had an important bearing on the life of Tony Perelli.

Mose was poor and a sycophant. To him Red was the biggest of Big Shots, a man in the automobile and silk shirt class. He gave to his more fortunate friend the reverence of subject to monarch. It was over a drink at the firm's speakeasy that Mose, gross of mind and body, offered information and a proposal.

Red shook his head.

'Chink girls don't mean nothing to me, Mose,' he said. 'Listen! There's a girl up town who's nuts about me! Joe Enrico's daughter, but I don't look at her twice. That's me, Mose.'

'Sure,' said Mose.

He looked twice at Minn Lee, and then more. He used to meet her on the stairs of the shabby apartment house where he had his home. She was Chinese and lovely. Small of stature, slim of body, with tiny, white hands that fascinated him. She was lovely—slanting brown eyes and skin like satin: when you saw it, you felt it. Her hair, not the blue-black of the Oriental but a sheeny black.

He used to give her a crooked grin. Then he tried to speak to her and found no difficulties. She was very simple and sweet and all too ready to talk. Her name was Minn Lee. Her husband was an artist, and a sick artist. She herself did fashion drawings.

Mose was staggered by her frank earnestness, and found no opportunity or opening for a more personal approach. Later, when he suggested supper at a swell place up town, she was more astonished than offended.

'But my husband is ill,' she said. 'I could not possibly leave him alone.'

'Aw, listen, baby! I'll fix it to have a woman come in and sit with him . . .'

She shook her head. When he fumbled for her hand it was not there—nor she.

After that she avoided him. He suspected that she watched out for his leaving the house before she went out to the market. To test this he left the house early one morning and waited at the end of the block. Presently he saw her and stood squarely in her path.

'Hey, angel-face! What's the idea? Keepin' out of my way?'

She was too honest to deny the charge, and tried to dodge past him, but he grabbed her.

'Wait a minute!'

He might have said much more, but a bony fist thumped him in the small of the back, and he spun round to stare into the merciless blue eyes of a man he had reason to detest. Sergeant Harrigan of the Central Office was laconic, offensively to the point.

'Hey, you! Leave that little Chinese girl alone, and tell me the story of your life, will you? That bit of your life that began at five last night and finished when you went to bed.'

Minn Lee slipped away like a frightened pigeon and was lost in the crowd.

'Why, Mr. Harrigan, I just don't know what you mean.' The voice of Mose became a plaintive and monotonous whine.

'Somebody stuck up a gentleman near Grant Park, took three hundred dollars and a watch from his pocket, and left him slumped on the sidewalk.'

'Why, Mr. Harrigan, I went to bed at ten . . .'

'You're a liar. You were seen near the Hippodrome at midnight. And you were seen near Grant Park at nine o'clock.'

11

There was a search of Mose Leeson's squalid little room and a personal search of Mose. All that day he alternated between police headquarters and the clinic to which the robbed and injured citizen had been taken. There was no identification, and Mose went free that night—relieved and wrathful.

Minn Lee heard all about it and was troubled. The dying artist who wailed at her from his neat bed demanded querulously what the hell she was thinking about and why she was making a meat soup for him and the day Friday. He had never had religion until he was ill. On the contrary, he favoured the more advanced school of thought which so heavily discounted the sacred symbols of divinity that they hardly had excuse for persisting. But since he had been sick he had ordered her to destroy certain drawings, notably the cartoon which caricatured so amusingly the Chicagoan's ideas of heaven. And all those nude studies of his, and certain appalling obscenities which had decorated the walls.

Minn Lee was neither glad nor sorry. These crude drawings meant nothing to her one way or the other. She recognised facts, but did not colour them nor tone them down. John Waite was a bad artist; she never thought that in his soul were the seeds of immortality. His perspectives were flat, his colour work was muddled, he had no sense of line, and even his drift towards vorticism, the last resort of all bad painters, had convinced nobody.

He was her man, that was all. Life and fate had linked them. There was reason enough for an infatuation which had the semblance of love, no reason at all for veneration. Yet she did not love him and did respect him. And he was dying. The German doctor had said so. Three months, maybe four. A priest came nowadays, a kindly man who was not shocked by the presence of Minn Lee, spoke to her humanly. He said three months too. There was a movement towards getting the painter to the coast, but nothing came of it. He protested vehemently against charity—he who had lived for years on an allowance made to him by the invalid mother he had brought to ruin. And when he was vehement he coughed and coughed and went on coughing all through the night.

12

The priest used to call twice a week. On the top floor he had another very sick man, who was also very old—Peter Melachini, sometime musician. He was not poor, but was as determined as any to die in the hovel which was his home. The slatternly wife of the plumber on the first floor told Minn Lee that old Peter was under the powerful protection of a Big Shot in the booze world.

'Can you beat it, Mrs. Waite? This guy offered to put Mr. Melachini in a grand house on the coast an' pay everything! But the old man wouldn't—no, ma'am, he said he'd stay right here in the city where he got born. He's crazy! A grand house on the coast an' everything!'

The Big Shot made occasional calls. Lithe, dark-faced men, nicely tailored, would suddenly appear in the street. Peering at them through dingy windows, the street grew pleasantly excited. Gunmen! Sure thing. Say, what an awful life—shoot'n' up folks, hey? They got as much as a hundred bucks a week. Yes, sir!

Then a dark car would sweep into the street and three men alight. One went first into the house, then the Big Shot himself, followed by the rear guard. He went straight up to Melachini's room, taking the basket of fruit from his henchman's hands.

' 'Lo, Peter—here's the works, boy.'

They had been in the same orchestra at Cosmolino's—Tony Perelli liked the old man. They were both Sicilian bred, both from a village outside Palermo.

Minn Lee met the Big Shot on the stairs. He was not tall, but carried himself with a certain dignity. His face was fleshy, his dark eyes held a spark of impish humour. He was heavily good-looking, perfectly fitted. About his waist was a belt with a diamond buckle. He smiled at Minn Lee, and she half smiled back. Looking over her shoulder after she had passed him, she saw him turn his head upward as though to take another look at her.

She saw him again in almost the same place, and he stopped and spoke to her. He was very polite, very kind, saw life from an amusing slant and made her laugh. He did not indulge in clumsy compliments, nor did he attempt to touch her hand.

The next day flowers and fruit came to the sick room.

13

On the fruiterer's label was written, 'From Tony Perelli', in a flourishing hand.

A Big Shot—my, what a Big Shot, breathed the plumber's wife. He's got the swellest apartment in Chicago. Cars, a country house an' everything. One of the Booze Lords, with a casualty list on what remained of his soul as long as Michigan Avenue, yes, ma'am!

Again Minn Lee was not shocked. People did odd things. In a way a booze racket was more decent than John Waite's peculiar art. Only she never made comparisons. The third time she saw Tony Perelli was when he called. Waite was asleep, and she admitted the visitor a little uneasily into the tiny sitting-room.

'Sleeping? Fine! I saw the doctor. He said your man should go to the coast. That crazy old Peter should go— but the hell he will! Listen, Mrs. Waite, if it's money . . .'

She shook her head. 'No, Mr. Perelli—he cannot take money because he cannot honourably return it,' she said. She used the word 'honourable' very often.

John Waite died a week later—died very quietly and unobtrusively, and when she had buried him and explained to the officials why her name was not Waite also, and had paid his immediate debts and had written to his mother, she set about finding work. It should have been easy for one who had a degree from Columbia University, and who had once earned as much as twenty-seven dollars and fifty cents in one week by drawing dresses for a ladies' magazine that no lady had ever seen, but she chose the easier way. There was a Chinese restaurant that needed girls. She wrote a business-like application to Che-foo Song, the proprietor, but before the answer came Mose Leeson called with a proposal.

The old Italian had died, and had been removed to an expensive funeral parlour. On the night he went to Carmel, Tony Perelli came to gather the dead man's belongings, and especially his family treasures. They were to go back to Sicily to a grandson and a grand-daughter.

Nobody saw Perelli, for he came on foot with his bodyguard before, beside and behind him. He passed swiftly into the house and glanced at Minn Lee's door as he went on his way.

The house was noisy tonight. On the second floor Laski the Polak, who had ambitions to be the world's champion trap-drummer, was making deafening and frilly sounds on his drum, to the distress and wrath of every tenant. Some say that his drum killed John Waite; it may have made death a sweet alternative.

If he could have seen the girl standing with white, drawn face in the grip of Mose Leeson ...

Mose was caveman by instinct. Experience helped him in the faith that women need to be carried off their feet.

'Honey, you can stand on what I say. I'll give you a swell time. I'm saying it! I'm nuts about you. . . .'

She struggled; she had to struggle. Tony Perelli heard the thin scream as he came down the stairs and tried the door. It yielded to his hand, and he went in.

'What do you want—wop?'

Mose was white-hot; his unpleasant face twitched convulsively as it was thrust into Perelli's.

'Beat it!'

Tony Perelli's voice was metallic, passionless.

'Beat it, eh? Sure I'll beat it—but not for no damn' Sicilian!'

His fist shot out; missed Perelli. The people in the other apartments heard only what sounded like a louder and more irregular beat of the drum.

Tony held the smoking pistol waist-high, but there was no need for a second shot. Mose had got his. He held for a second to the bedrail, then slipped down to the floor.

Minn Lee looked gravely from killed to killer.

'Get your coat and come away.'

Perelli's orders could never be mistaken for requests. She obeyed and went out with him along the street and into his waiting car. The men he left behind would deal adequately with Mose Leeson. There would be no fuss; the situation was far from being unusual, and would develop normally. A car driver found his body lying on the prairie in the snow; the newspapers said 'Another Gang Shooting', and that was the end of it.

In the meantime Minn Lee had gone to the home of Tony and became accustomed to being addressed as Mrs. Perelli.

15

2

From the broad balcony with its venetian balustrading
Tony Perelli could look down upon the city which he was
to rule. He loved Chicago, every stone of it.

Chicago was home and kingdom. The endless trails of
cars which passed up and down the broad avenue beneath
him bore his subjects to their daily work—his subjects and
his partners. Beneath every one of those shiny roofs was a
man or woman who kept 'the best' in their cellars. Visitors
who came to dinner would have the best brought to the
table—the best in gilt-necked bottles, the best in sparkling
decanters.

It was against the law that the best should be made or
sold at all; every furtive case or keg smuggled into the cellars stood for lawlessness, every purchaser contributed to
the smuggler who purveyed it and the gunman who pro-
tected it. Rather than that they should be denied the satisfaction of parading the best upon their tables, they tacitly
agreed that any person interfering with its delivery should
be shot and flung from a moving car on to the roadside.
They would have been horrified at the suggestion, but they
paid for the shells that wiped these vexatious people from
the face of the earth, and unconsciously subscribed to the
flowers that went to their funerals.

Perelli went back to the glorious salon which was at
once breakfast-room, living-room and drawing-room. Snif-
fing and superior critics who had seen it likened it to the
entrance hall of a super cinema. They spoke of it as vulgar
and garish and tawdry. It was in truth an exact replica of
the most beautiful room in the Palace of the Doge.

Kiki, his Japanese servant, had brought his coffee. Minn
Lee, in obedience to the routine he had established and

16

which later he was to relax, would not be visible before the afternoon. Angelo had recently rented an apartment in a fashionable area, and would not appear till later.

He looked at his watch. Eight o'clock. Not too early for a caller. He had heard the purr of the signal bell and knew exactly who that caller was.

Red Gallway was never quite comfortable in this environment; he was even less comfortable this morning, because he had a grievance and found it difficult to maintain the overnight fury into which he had been worked.

'Sit down, Red. Tell me all that is happening on the West Side, huh?'

Red swallowed.

'It's what happenin' in Chicago that beats me,' he said huskily. 'I gotta know somep'n', Perelli—if I don't know I'll start somep'n'—see?'

Perelli regarded him from under his long lashes curiously. He might have favoured some unusual animal with a similar scrutiny.

'Start something? Funny! You make me laff! Start something. Well? Start!'

Red moved uncomfortably in the chair on which he sat.

'That guy Leeson—Mose Leeson. Him and me was friends, Perelli. Somebody bumped him. Say, I'd like to meet that guy.'

Antonio Perelli smiled.

'I bumped him,' he said simply.

There was an awkward silence.

'Well?'

Red's face was twisted ludicrously.

'Say—that's no way to treat a regular feller . . . friend of mine . . . me and Mose is like brothers.'

'Then you should be in mourning,' said Perelli calmly, 'for your brother is dead.'

'Why?'

Red jerked out the query with an effort. There was no reply.

'Say, what's the idea? Mose was a right man. He's been useful to me.'

Protest of some sort was called for.

'I thought I would.'

Tony Perelli was perched on the wooden settle in front of the organ which stood in one corner of the room. He picked up the coffee by his side and sipped thoughtfully.

'Yes—I thought I would. I guess when I feel that way I just do what I want.'

Red licked his dry lips. Inwardly he quaked and raged alternately.

'Well, it don't seem you've done right by me, Perelli—tha's all.'

Tony nodded.

'Yeh! I sympat'ise. It is very understandable. Have you been to hospital? No? A friend of yours is there—Antropolos the Greek. He is feeling very sore. Somebody beat him up last night. Why, you ask? I see that you do not. He was beaten up because he sold coke to one of my boys. Hey? That is good news or bad?'

The other man did not answer.

'They shall not drink, they shall not sniff the coke, or do things which make their 'eads go funny and their 'ands go so!'

His outstretched hand trembled artistically.

'I guess I can look after myself . . .' began Red.

'Sure you can. And who cares if you don't? But you are not paid to look after yourself. You are paid to look after me and my boys. If your 'and shakes and your 'ead goes zooey, that is bad, and if you talk when you booze that is worse, but worst of all is this, that a hophead will spill his friends' secrets to buy more hop. So that is all.'

'Listen . . .'

'That is all. Cut out that white stuff or quit.'

Red rose to his feet.

'That's O.K. by me,' he said. 'I'll quit!'

Again that swift, sly smile.

'Sure. Quit!'

Dull in most respects, Red recognised the menace in that last word and wilted.

'Listen, Tony. I'm a guy that doesn't like to be pushed around—say, I'm not a child, and don't you forget it! If two guys can't get together they oughter quit. Tha's all.'

Tony nodded.

'That's all,' he said.

So Red went, his head buzzing with plans, for he now knew certain ends of the booze racket that he had not known before, and would never have known but for Tony Perelli's instruction. He sought out a member of the gang with whom he was on terms of sympathy, and over lunch at Bellini's poured into his ears the story of his grievances.

Victor Vinsetti was a well-dressed young man with restless eyes; he seemed everlastingly expecting to find somebody behind him. His own views he rarely expressed, but he was a good and ready listener. And so he listened.

He learned of Red's little quarrel, and of Mose, and how easy it would be to run a separate racket, get booze in over the frontier, cut it and find a market. And how, with a few good boys to persuade the speakeasies, one could come to fortune in a ludicrously short space of time. Vinsetti listened interestedly, because he himself had held such opinions. As for himself, he had formed his own plans.

'So you see, Vic,' said Red at long last.

'Sure, I see—but it's not so easy, Red—and anyway, you're a bonehead to talk like you're talking.'

'Mose was a square shooter . . .'

'Mose was just nothing and then not,' said Vinsetti calmly. 'He's dead, and it's no loss to the United States or the cause of Pure Government. He was just a vote. Next election you can poll twice and he'll be alive. No. I wonder what Perelli thinks about it?'

He pondered this while Red surveyed him curiously. For Vinsetti was a near-Big Shot, reputedly wealthy. And rumour did not lie. Vinsetti was an 'outer'. He was prepared to give the lie to tradition that once you were 'in' you could never 'get out'. His cabin was reserved on the *Empress of Australia*, for he planned to leave via Canada; his share stock had been liquidated and was now currency. Already he had negotiated for a seashore house at San Remo. Red's frankness was a little alarming—and at Bellini's, where every other waiter was a spy.

That night he saw Perelli.

'Red's sore,' he said, 'and he's talking. He stuck me in Bellini's with a whole bellyful of aches.'

'I don't want no trouble,' said Tony Perelli. It was at once his slogan and alibi.

19

But Red, all lit up, was for bad trouble. Brilliant ideas were flowing in upon him. Through an intermediary he sought Mike Feeney, Baron of the South Side. He got no further than Shaun O'Donnell, who was Mike's chief of staff by appointment and brother by marriage.

But Shaun was the real leader, the brains of the outfit. ('That's the worst thing that's ever been said about Mike Feeney's crowd,' Perelli was to say on a subsequent occasion.) Shaun was small thin, irritable, too quick on the draw for some, too mouthily offensive for others. He listened to Red's propasals coldly and gave him no encouragement.

'Red, you're no darn good to us or nobody,' he said with rude frankness. 'You're a hophead and you booze. I'm telling you, boy. We got no room in this outfit for guys who sniff. Perelli's a this and that, but we don't want no trouble with him. If you break into his territory we'll help you with the Best Stuff.'

'Mose . . .' began Red.

'Mose can stay plumb in hell where he b'longs,' said Shaun.

The next day nothing much happened. The temperature of Red Gallway's feet went down some forty degrees, and in the dusk of a wintry afternoon he sidled into police headquarters and demanded an interview with Chief Kelly. He wanted to make a complaint about a policeman. He said this very loudly, because police headquarters was in Perelli's area, and inside and out there were watchful eyes and attentive ears.

Nobody but Red would have gone to police headquarters; they would have followed the usual procedure of phoning and fixing an appointment for a secret meeting. Red—who when he was lit up had no finesse—took the bold step, and a quarter of an hour after he arrived he was talking to the grim-faced chief of detectives.

His version would have been that he spoke cleverly, avoided mentioning names. The only thing he was certain about was that his life was in danger, and after he had spoken for a little while Mr. Kelly was even more certain than he on the subject.

Red was not clever, he was not particularly well guarded. Actually he did not spell out names and dot the i's. He told

20

Kelly nothing he did not know. The chief knew by bitter experience that if he held the man as a witness and put him on the stand before a jury, he would retract every word he had spoken, that if he were to sign a written statement he would swear with the greatest fervour that that statement had been secured by a trick, or by bullying, or by threats of physical violence, or whilst he was unconscious as the result of such physical violence.

The chief knew just how Mose had died and why. He knew the names of the men who had taken his body away, and the number of the car they had used. The latter was easy: they had found the car, a stolen one, abandoned.

Red would have continued talking all through the night, but the chief was busy, and he hated one-sided conversation that told him nothing.

'Do you want me to keep you inside?' he asked.

Red was indignant.

'What, me? I guess I can look after myself. No, sir! I'm going out of Chicago tomorrow. I'm through. I've got some friends out east who'll stake me to all the money I want.'

There was a stage in Red's intoxication when he acquired rich supporters; he had reached this.

He went out on to the street with three shadows behind him. Two of them were police officers.

'Don't lose sight of that bird,' was the chief's instruction.

He had not gone a block when two men fell in with Red, one on each side of him.

'Say, what the . . .' began Red, when they locked their arms affectionately in his.

'You squawk and you go dead,' said one of them pleasantly.

He stuck a snub-nosed belly gun into the side of the prisoner.

'Step out, you . . . !'

The detectives walking behind were new to the game. They saw only the arrival of two close friends of their quarry, and when the three came abreast of a waiting car and got in, their man in the front seat by the driver, his two companions in the back, they did no more than look around for a taxi. Before one drew up to them the car had gone ahead and was out of sight.

Red did not quite realise what was happening. You may sober a man who is suffering from alcholism, but one who is lit with dope is not so readily brought back to normality. The only thing he was perfectly certain about was that the man sitting immediately behind him in the car was pushing something hard against the back of his neck, and was chatting pleasantly across the seat with the driver. They were talking about a ball game, and argued hotly whether Southern California would beat Notre Dame or vice versa. The driver was all for Notre Dame, gave reasons why it should win, reeled off long lists of previous victories and performances, and offered to bet a hundred dollars on the team of his choice, which the man sitting immediately behind him instantly took.

'I'm all for Notre Dame,' said Red.

'You shut your mouth,' said the driver, 'and keep it shut. I wonder your throat's not sore, the time you've been squawking to the bulls.'

'Me squawk?' protested Red indignantly.

The gun muzzle at his neck thumped painfully into the back of his head.

'Shut up.'

They left the town behind; dreary stretches of country ran past on either side, with an occasional house. Presently they came to a little plantation by the side of the bumpy road. The driver stopped.

'Step out,' he said, and Red stepped.

The drug had worn off. He was shaking from head to foot.

'Say, what's the big idea?' he quavered. 'I've done no squawking. You take me right back to Tony. . . .'

With a man on each arm he lurched across the rough ground, past the first outlying trees.

'You're not going to bump me off, are you?' His voice was a thin whine. 'Listen—I've done nothing.'

The man behind him thumbed back the hammer of his revolver and fired. Red went down on his knees, swayed. He heard neither the first nor the second shot. The executioner put the gun in his pocket and lit a cigarette. The flame of his match did not quiver.

'Let's go,' he said.

22

He took the place that Red had occupied, and half-way back to town the argument of Southern California against Notre Dame was resumed.

The driver saw the squad car, above the whirr of his own engine heard the squeal of its siren. He jerked the car round and stepped on the accelerator.

'Get the typewriter—it's under the seat.'

The other man crawled over his shoulder. They let down the back flap and poked out the muzzle of the machine-gun.

'The coppers must have got Kelly on the wire,' said the executioner, who had seen the shadows that were following Red.

The car was getting closer.

'Let her have it,' he said, and the machine-gun man pressed the trigger.

Rat-a-tat-a-tat-a-tat-a-tat!

The windscreen of the pursuing car was smashed. It swerved slightly, then came up. Three pencils of flame shot out. The machine-gun fired again. The driver of the car behind made a wild swerve and the burst missed.

'Hell!' said the man with the machine-gun, and again rested the barrel on the back of the car, steadied it with his hand, then slid gently to the floor.

The gun poised for a moment, then fell backward on to the road. There was a sharp report: the police car had struck the weapon, and one of the tyres had ripped off. The assassin looked back through the flap.

'Ditched,' he said. 'Go to it, Joe.'

He took a small torch from his pocket and flashed it on to the figure huddled on the floor. In the centre of his forehead was a big, red, ugly hole. The man climbed back to his place beside the driver.

'That bet of yours is phoney,' he said. 'Billy has got his.'

All the way back to town they talked of the coming ball game, and the inert thing behind them rolled and rocked with every corner they took.

Vinsetti was no ordinary gangster, held no ordinary position. For two years he had been the suave ambassador, the plenipotentiary travelling from coast to coast, the go-between who crossed and re-crossed the lakes to Canada. At times he had been a high-grade negotiator and settled differences which threatened to develop gruesomely if gang leaders kept their promise.

He was a good-looking young man, had a reputation for gallantry, and harboured the illusion of invincibility. There was certain justification for this.

But he made the mistake of engaging himself in Canada to a young lady who did not accept her ultimate dismissal with good grace. One day, when Vinsetti went across to Toronto to fix a delivery of whisky, a lawyer's emissary slipped a writ into his hand. He was sued for breach of promise, and even more than that. Vinsetti had no cosmopolitan sense of law. It was a matter to be fixed and he looked around for a fixer, choosing a disreputable lawyer who accepted his fee, made one half-hearted effort to secure a withdrawal of the action and, when he failed, forgot all about it. The consequence was that Vinsetti was cast in heavy damages, and on his next visit to Toronto was arrested. He paid because he had to pay; but that was not the worst; he ceased to be buying agent, suffered a very considerable cut of his revenue.

'I don't want no trouble,' said Tony Perelli when the matter was discussed. 'You're in bad with these Canadian guys. I don't want people working for me who are rubbered on the street.'

'I don't see how it affects you,' said Vinsetti, inwardly boiling.

Tony stroked his little moustache and studied the pattern of his silky carpet.

'Maybe not,' he said. 'Maybe that girl didn't squeal before the judge, and say you was in a whisky racket and was making a million dollars. Maybe she didn't say you was working with Antonio Perelli. That's bad.' He shook his head. 'You go east, Victor mio, there's plenty to do, plenty money, plenty fun. I am not sore—it is a bad break, but I am not sore.'

He patted Vinsetti's shoulder gently.

That evening, sitting alone with Minn Lee, he opened his heart to her. He sat by her side on a silken divan in that big salon of his; the golden gates were wide open, and the delicately scented apartment lay bathed in the soft radiance of amber lamps.

'That guy is too fond of women, and making love and such nonsense.'

'Is it nonsense?' she asked, and he smiled.

'To you, my sweet peach blossom, no, but where in the world is another you, hey?'

He dropped her little hand on her lap, strolled across to the big organ that stood in one corner of the room, and played continuously for an hour, and she listened, entranced. He was a beautiful musician, a violinist of considerable ability, but the organ was his passion. He would sit for hours, extemporising, bringing in all the scraps of Italian opera that he remembered. Italian opera was the beginning and end of art for Tony Perelli. He loathed jazz, although he danced extraordinarily well.

For an hour Minn Lee sat, in her new satin robe, legs crossed like a little Buddha, her hands folded meekly, her head bent. When Tony came back to her and lounged on the sofa by her side, he spoke again of Vinsetti.

'That boy is too clever; yet he is very useful. It was a bad break, but everybody must have a bad break sometimes. Perhaps he is yellow—I do not know. Victor lives too softly —that takes the devil out of a man. But he doesn't drink, and he doesn't talk, and he's got a swell way with swell people.'

Victor's lapse was overlooked a few days later when he negotiated with Chief Kelly for the release of a man who was being held—unjustly, as it happened—for an offence under the Mann Act. The individual so held was of immediate value to Tony, and his release was something of a triumph for the lieutenant.

'I should have held that guy,' said Chief Detective Kelly, when he and Harrigan were discussing the matter.

'There's got to be a lot of give and take in this business, Chief,' said Harrigan. 'My own opinion is that Perelli worked his release because he was afraid of us fastening another crime on him—they found Red Gallway this morning, by the way—plugged through the back.'

Kelly nodded.

'That was always coming to him. A loud speaker, that

25

bird; sooner or later he'd have blown wide. It's a waste of time, but you might see Perelli.' He scratched his chin irritably. 'No, I guess I'll see him myself.'

'There's a new lady up at his apartment.'

'I know—Minn Lee. Mrs. Waite, or whatever her name was. If there's any honour amongst thieves, Perelli has it all. He's got the tightest bunch of hoodlums in the town. We've never had a squeal from any of his regular gang.'

Harrigan looked at him oddly.

'There's one who'll come across sooner or later,' he said, lowering his voice.

Kelly pursed his lips.

'Vinsetti—I wonder? If there was a chance of it, Perelli would know first, and if Perelli knew first . . .'

He smiled.

Harrigan bit off the end of a cigar and lit it.

'He'll never take the stand—none of them will—but he's copper-hearted and he'll give us the dope on a whole lot of things that'll be mighty useful for the file.'

Again Kelly shook his head, and again he said:

'I wonder? Do you see Vinsetti often?' he asked. 'You might put him right on one point. Perelli knows he's quitting and it's pretty unhealthy when a man takes a powder on Perelli. Perhaps if he knows this he'll come across. We'll give him protection—put him right on board the boat. Anyway, the gang wouldn't start anything in Canada—the laws are still working there.'

Harrigan spent the next two days fixing up an accidental meeting with Victor Vinsetti, and he failed for the excellent reason that Vinsetti had seen Minn Lee and was aflame.

Certain things to Minn Lee were honourable and certain things dishonourable. It was dishonourable to deceive your man; it was honourable to betray all for his sake. Vinsetti's calls were reported, all he said, all he did, all that he proposed. In his queer way Perelli was flattered by the attention she excited. He grew ecstatic over her loyalty, for she had told him simply, as one relating everyday events, not in a spirit of boastfulness, nor coyly, nor yet to inspire his pleasant jealousy.

Vinsetti had spoken about many things: Love, for example, devotion, the splendour of life in Europe. But he had said other things which were disturbing to Antonio Perelli's sense of dignity. For example, those houses in Cicero—she had never heard of them before, was not shocked even now. If she had gone into Che-foo Song's restaurant, where Chinese girls danced—well, there was not much difference between Cicero and the smoke-laden atmosphere of the Stars of Heaven Restaurant.

No, she was not shocked; a little startled, just a little hurt; for this man had suddenly become as a god to her.

Tony was both shocked and hurt; when he met Vinsetti the next day, his manner was curt, and at the end of the business interview . . .

'When Minn Lee wants to see you she will get you on the wire, Victor,' he said. 'You're a swell fellow but you talk too much. . . . Oh no, not of love, but of Cicero, eh? You made a grand hit—but not with me, Victor.'

Looking into his eyes, Vinsetti saw the red light, and yet those eyes were kind and good-humoured, and that thick mouth of Tony Perelli's was curled in a grin.

But the red light was there; Vinsetti sensed it.

You might quarrel with Tony Perelli, lash him to a fury, but if the subject of the quarrel did not make contact with the basic facts of life, when the trouble was over you went on just as you were. Your offence and his were forgiven and forgotten. Within a certain fenced area the quarrel might become a battle royal and no harm come of it, but outside the boundary line was death, quick, merciless —expedient.

Expediency governed every move, every action, every thought. Let any man impinge upon the safety line, open or threaten to open one stronghold door, and he vanished in the dark. As yet Tony Perelli's quarrel with him was purely domestic. His dignity had been hurt; he had been lowered in the eyes of his woman. He would destroy no man for that. Still, Vinsetti saw the red light and became cold and cautious and watchful. He had the mind of a diplomat, and the most powerful weapon in the diplomat's armoury is to impress upon his antagonist the sense of the reactions most flattering to him. So Vinsetti sulked, pretended more to being the guilty lover than the treacher-

27

ous comrade, and after a while it seemed that the situation
came back to normal. Not so with Vinsetti. Perhaps he had
seen too much: he had certainly imagined more than was
good for his peace of mind.

Tony was unusually generous. There was something of
the cat in him; he preferred to strike brusquely and without warning. Now he warned. The next time Vinsetti called
at the apartment, Perelli made a suggestion.

'There will be no vacation for you this year, Victor,' he
said. 'I guess I'd sell that reservation on the *Empress of
Australia*—why waste money?'

Just that, no more. No recriminations, no reproaches,
no cold fury at this unforgivable act. For the man who
takes a powder on the gang is outcast; and if he is detected after he has made his getaway, all manner of troubles
await him. Notifications go forward through a strangely
active police that the man is a criminal; foreign ports are
barred against him; he may land only to be arrested, and
possibly deported, and a man so deported would go back,
as he knew, to waiting guns.

Perelli had an espionage system which was well-nigh per-
fect. He had clerks in the banks who furnished him with
particulars about his own people. He knew to a cent their
balances, would be instantly informed about the transfer
of money or stock to another country, and particularly did
he keep tag of cheques drawn in favour of travel agencies
or steamship companies.

Vinsetti was one of the few men who kept a banking
account. As a rule gangsters do not trust banks, rather
putting their faith in safe deposit boxes. Tony could keep
watch, therefore, on the more intimate side of Victor Vinsetti's life. He knew all about the letter of credit that the
bank had sold him. His chief offence was that attack at
Cicero. Somebody had tipped off Mike and his friends, and
here was the natural sequel. Three men alone knew of the
forthcoming visit—certainly not the trader in Canada, who
had no idea that his lucrative customer was Tony Perelli.
It was a great pity about Vinsetti, Angelo agreed, for he
was a wise boy and an asset; one must have fellows who
could dress well to deal with those honest and respectable
villains who supplied the raw material of Mr. Perelli's trade.

As a liaison officer between the outfits he was unrivalled. Vinsetti could walk into any territory and get away without so much as a smell of powder. He was *persona grata* with Joe the Polak, Mike Feeney and various other members of the various organisations. He was discreet, could be relied upon to keep his word, was the gangman's idea of a square shooter. It was, as Angelo Verona said, a great pity.

Events were moving in one inevitable direction. Perelli's activities were multifarious; he had fingers in all makes and shapes of pies, some legitimate, some distinctly illicit. He kept rigidly aloof from the ordinary criminal classes. He neither financed nor benefited by vulgar robbery with or without violence. The monies of men who fell victim to his vengeance or suspicion were invariably found intact. Sometimes enormous sums were discovered in the pockets of the dead men left derelict by the roadside. He kept faith with seller and buyer; his word was his bond, and he even resented the practice of sending the booze he supplied to the analyst. His wages bill was enormous, his turnover colossal. Though he maintained a small army of accountants and clerks, he carried all the details of his transactions in his head.

Greatest of his gifts was a sixth sense which warned him of danger. When that alarum sounded in his mind he accepted no excuses, but obeyed the warning blindly. Generally the reason he gave for some swift act of retribution was not the real reason. Red had been killed ostensibly for a visit to the police station. He died not because of the immediate but because of the future danger.

3

If Perelli punished ruthlessly, his rewards were on the side
of munificence. He spent fifty thousand dollars in furnish-
ing Angelo's new apartment—a bungling recruit to gangdom who had saved his life he sent back to Sicily a rich
man; he was too awkward a gunman to retain, too brave a
man to be dismissed.

Vinsetti? Perelli thought a lot about Vinsetti. He was
independent, had lost his old enthusiasms, possessed a
grievance. Vinsetti had a very sensitive reception and received in full the tonal disharmonies of Perelli's mind.
Through one agent he wrote, cancelling his berth on the
Empress of Australia, and through another agent booked
the same accommodation in another name. Which was
exactly what Tony Perelli thought he would do.

The fascinations of Minn Lee had not dissipated: Victor
Vinsetti sent her flowers, wrote little notes to her, very
clever little notes, and poetical. Tony read them smilingly.

'Victor is a swell writer—ask him to call again, Minn
Lee. . . . Sure I don't mind! I like it . . . he's a swell feller and
very funny.'

So Minn Lee wrote in her neat schoolgirl hand, and
Vinsetti came and drank tea with her, and sometimes Tony
was there, but more often he was not.

There might be urgent need for Victor Vinsetti very
soon. He shone as an arbitrator. The two big gangs were
edging across neutral ground into one another's territory.

Feeney's crowd supplied a large number of speakeasies
on the north side with hard liquor and beer. Mike ran a
couple of breweries and was a millionaire. There was a
sort of no-man's-land on this battlefield, where both gangs
operated side by side. The proprietors of the speakeasies

might buy safety from one side or the other. There was no 'you take ours or none' in the tactics of either party. Then suddenly Mike changed front, claimed the territory as being exclusively his own and passed out the customary warnings, which were followed by the customary reprisals. One of Perelli's good customers had his establishment wrecked and was himself beaten up. He hastened to Angelo with the story of rapine, and Angelo reported.

'Let Victor see this mick,' said Perelli. 'Who did the beating?'

They told him it was one Death House Hennesey, a notorious strong-arm man who had operated with his personal gang. He was a sub-contractor of violence very often employed by Shaun O'Donnell when the Irishman did not wish to be identified with a foray or find it expedient to detach details from his main bodyguard.

'Give Hennesey the works,' said Perelli, 'but let Victor see Feeney or O'Donnell.'

Victor went down to a certain hotel near North State and interviewed the irritable little Irishman. Shaun O'Donnell was not amenable to reason; he was truculent and breathed vague threats. Vinsetti, in his best diplomatic style, sought a *modus vivendi*, but Shaun, who had never heard the expression—and, if he had, would have disapproved of it—was adamant.

'Listen, Vic—that territory has always been ours and you can tell Mister Perelli that it stays ours. We stood for his muscle, but now the Polaks are crowding us we gotta tighten up. You're a swell feller, Vic, and me and Mike would go the coast to oblige you, but fair's fair.'

There were other negotiations, and in the course of these Shaun said:

'I wonder a guy like you stays around with the Perelli outfit. Mike 'n' me would be glad to see you with a place in our organisation. I know!'—when Vinsetti protested—'you're all plumb scared of Perelli, but suppose we was tipped off about some place where we could find him, hey? That guy treats men like dogs.'

Crude temptation, but Victor pondered it. And in the meantime Death House Hennesey got the works.

A car drove up to the door of his little house and somebody rang the bell. Hennesey opened the door and peered into the night. . . .

A distant motorcyclist policeman heard the rattle of machine-gun fire and streaked towards the sound. Death House Hennesey was slumped over the balustrade of his porch with twenty machine-gun slugs in his physical system.

Shaun O'Donnell accepted the fact philosophically. It meant nothing in his life that a sub-contractor had gone. There were others who charged less. Still, it was a peg on which to hang an attack on Perelli. He personally paid for Hennesey's funeral and attended the lying in state. Perelli sent a wreath; and such was his power that the men who hated him, and who knew that he had encompassed the death of the man to whose pious memory the flowers paid tribute, dared not displace them.

To Minn Lee he spoke freely; he kept fewer secrets from her than from any woman who had entered and vanished from his life.

'In this racket, sweetheart, there are four points to the compass, and a guy that goes half-way between north 'n' west gets nowhere on his own feet. Victor is a swell talker, but he ain't talked over Shaun O'Donnell, and another of my speakeasies was broken up last night. And yet Victor does not say "Go to it!" All he says is "Wait, wait," and, by God, I wait and see my business go to hell!'

Victor had reason for saying 'wait'. He saw Tony and reported negotiations, and the Big Shot listened patiently.

'Sure that's fine!' he said. 'Maybe I wait till Shaun O'Donnell gets an old man and has sense, huh? For ten years maybe! This mick must settle or he gets the works, Victor—I'm saying it! There is too much talk—let Ricardo speak.'

Ricardo was his favourite machine-gun chopper; a man who had fought in the Great War and had three decorations and twenty killings to his name.

'I will wait a little longer—yes,' said Perelli, 'and then . . .'

He drove out to Cicero that afternoon, and was sitting in his own restaurant, sipping coffee, when three cars drove slowly past and swept the restaurant with machine-gun fire. Perelli lay flat on the floor in a confusion of smashed glass and falling plaster, and decided that he could not afford to wait: he must move, and move quickly.

The attack had not been improvised: it was the result of careful planning. Vinsetti was one of the very few who knew that he was going to Cicero on that particular day—Victor had actually planned the trip, the object of which was to meet a Canadian shipper.

He made enquiries. Mike Feeney and Shaun had left on the previous night for New York; their alibi was a little too cleverly established.

He saw Victor on his return and was very voluble about the narrowness of his escape. To have made light of the matter would have been a mistake. Vinsetti would have been alarmed, and who knew what a frightened rat might do?

Victor was alarmed, nevertheless. He sent an urgent message to Kelly, and had an interview with the Chief, giving him a little information but promising more. Then Vinsetti did a curious thing—it was one of those bizarre acts of his that were peculiar to the man. He called at his lawyer's and made a will, one clause of which ran:

In the event of my dying by violence and on the coroner's verdict that murder has been committed I direct that the sum of one hundred thousand dollars shall be set aside from my estate as a reward to the person who shall secure the conviction of my murderer and his execution.

In the afternoon he called on Minn Lee. She had phoned an invitation to tea at Tony's suggestion.

'You may stay in your suite, little darling,' he said, 'for I have much business to finish with Victor.'

Vinsetti called at 4.30. A quarter of an hour later Kelly came. This was the arrangement which had been agreed between them. In truth the detective arrived outside the entrance of the building five minutes after Vinsetti went in, and filled the idle time by watching some men load furniture on a truck. Two big chairs, a davenport, a coat-rack and a table were loaded and pulled away as Kelly entered the building and made for the elevator.

Angelo opened the door to him.

'Victor's gone,' he said. 'He only stayed a minute—came to see Minn Lee, Chief, but she's got a headache.'

'Where's Perelli?'

He was on the sun balcony, and was sent for.

'Vinsetti came in here fifteen minutes ago and he couldn't have gone,' said Kelly unpleasantly.

'If he is not here he could have gone,' he said. 'There are two ways out, Chief—one at the back of the block—Victor usually goes that way.'

'I'd like to search this apartment.'

Kelly was frankly and rudely sceptical.

'Sure!' Tony Perelli was all smiles.

Vinsetti was gone—how, whither, was a mystery. Kelly knew of the back exit and had had a man stationed there, but Victor Vinsetti had not passed.

Two days later they found his body floating in the lake. He had been shot dead at close quarters, and in his pocket were eighty sodden notes, each for a thousand dollars.

They hauled Perelli down to police headquarters and quizzed him.

'I hope you get the guy that bumped poor Victor,' he said. 'There's too much of these killings.'

He attended the funeral, riding in an armoured car just behind the funeral coach.

Vinsetti was something of a litterateur. He kept a big diary which, to the disappointment of Chief Kelly, and to the infinite relief of at least one person, contained no vital information.

On a visit to Hollywood he had made this illuminating comment:

'The gangster's life has no continuity. It is a series of short stories written round the same funeral parlour. . . . New characters appear on the stage and vanish, almost before they have established their identity. . . . The story of gangland is punctuated with shootings by machine-guns, and most of the punctuation marks are full stops.'

The diary was in Italian, and Chief Kelly, reading a translation, enlarged his philosophy but did not extend the volume of his files.

Minn Lee saw gangland from her own peculiar angle.

She met men and women who came and went, and sometimes reappeared. The women were pretty, rather loud of voice, expensively dressed and jewelled. They seemed perfectly happy in their environment, which perhaps was an improvement on the life they had previously known.

Tony was kind to her, much kinder than John Waite had been. He showed her consideration, a pleasing tenderness and a large understanding.

Once a girl came from Cicero to lunch with them. Her attitude towards Perelli was familiar, and yet the familiarity was tinged with a certain reserve which might have meant respect or fear, and probably had in it something of both. She was pretty in a coarse way, had a sable stole and elegant rings.

She drank incessantly throughout lunch, and her conversation was more or less Greek to Minn Lee. She knew the place, too; looked round it with a proprietorial smirk, appraised Minn Lee in one sweeping, searching glance, and thereafter ignored her; except that towards the end of lunch she leaned over and took Minn Lee's hand and examined the big ring.

'You want to be careful of that baby,' she said. 'It's a bum cut, and the stone slips out of its setting.'

Looking up, she caught Tony's glance and dropped the girl's hand as though it were red hot. But Minn Lee was no fool. The woman had worn this ring, and in her crude way was acquainting its new proprietor with the important fact.

Any reserve Tony might have maintained was shaken down by this incident. He began to ask questions about the jewellery the visitor was wearing, where it had come from, how much it had cost. It was a little embarrassing, both for Minn Lee and the person to whom the queries were addressed. Apparently they had been given to her by various 'boys'. She named Vinsetti.

'Because he's dead?' asked Perelli quietly. 'Tell me the names of some live men who gave you those things.'

She was confused, went red, then white, tried to carry off the situation with a laugh and a wisecrack, but Perelli drove through all her flippancy.

'You should be very careful, Enid,' he said, that metallic

35

tang in his voice. 'You have a good job, yes? And receipts are falling very severely.'

She came back with a whine about the vigilants and the difficulties of finding the right people—a tactful move apparently, for Perelli changed the subject with an abruptness which would have been offensive to any other woman.

He would not speak about her to Minn Lee. After she had gone:

'She is nobody—just trash,' he said. 'Once she stayed here, but she was too fresh for me, and she laughed at my music, because she has no brain—just a face and a line of flip talk, and she bored me. I hate people who bore me, little Minn Lee.'

She smiled quietly at him.

'I wonder if I ever shall?' she asked.

He took her hand and kissed it.

'When I am very, very old,' he said. 'That is possible. When I do not like lovely things and lovely voices and all that is good for the eyes.'

He took her head in his two hands.

'Are you 'appy?' And, when she nodded, he lifted her on to his knee and, taking her in his arms, nursed her like a child without speaking; and in the comfort of that caress his mind was soothed and expanded, and he could give undivided, dispassionate attention to the problem of Shaun O'Donnell and the Feeney crowd. For they were getting on his nerves.

Mike Feeney was big, awkwardly built, a typical mick of a man, who had started life as an excavator and, having secured control of a trade union, had multiplied its membership to an amazing extent by the simple process of beating up every man who refused to join. To his credit it must be said that he had secured concessions for his members, for he was one of the initiators of the pineapple method of persuasion. A pineapple is a bomb; and a bomb placed on the porch of an employer who refused to accept the conditions which Mike and his executives dictated usually brought about a change of heart in a very short time. If it did not, then the next bomb was more destructive. Few employers waited for the second pineapple; none stood out for the third.

36

The booze racket offered golden opportunities. He had all the machinery for terrorisation. His speakeasies appeared overnight—strange little dives, some of them; elaborately furnished others. He supplied them with booze; his gun squad grew in importance. He opened gaming houses, pool rooms, muscled in to the handbook industry, which is a euphemism for bookmaking.

His sister, Mrs. Shaun O'Donnell, played an important part in the organisation. She was a driving force and, through her husband, the executive of the outfit. Almost as tall as her brother, big-boned, gaunt, red-faced, with hands like raw meat and a nose which was long and permanently red, this big-footed lady had once, so it was said, fought a man and beaten him. Nobody ever questioned this. Mike Feeney in his cups boasted of it.

With all the money in the world, she was the worst-dressed woman in Chicago. She affected flaming violets, impossible reds, wore diamonds as big as nuts, set in gold brooches the size of coffee saucers. Her voice rasped and rasped, and when she spoke the Feeney crowd stirred uncomfortably.

Perelli she hated for his very masculine qualities. To her he was always 'the wop dude'. She called him other names, for she did not approve of those houses at Cicero. When her history comes to be written it will be found that she urged her husband to inaugurate rival establishments.

She ruled her husband rather than her brother, which was remarkable, for Shaun had a temper of his own and the brain of three Mike Feeneys. For the rest, she was as remorseless as any; sent men to their death and never thought of them again. It was she who organised an attack on Tony Perelli.

'We surely scared that peterman,' she said to her husband. 'If you had the heart of a man you'd go and get him, after what he said about me to Mrs. Merlo. Maybe it don't mean nothin' to you, having your wife called "Romeo's nightmare!" But if that don't mean something insulting I'm a crazy woman! Go get that wop, Shaun!'

Shaun snarled round at her.

'You're in a hell of a hurry to get rid of me, ain't ye?' he snapped. 'You keep outa this, Bella.'

She had been named by an unimaginative parent Flori-
bella.

News of the beautiful Chinese girl who was staying at
Perelli's apartment reached her, and feminine curiosity
took her calling. She towered above little Minn Lee like an
ugly derrick above an Easter lily. For once in her life she
was human. Perelli was amazed to learn that she had left
a good impression on the girl. As for Mrs. O'Donnell . . .

'That baby's too good to live in a place like that with a
dirty little Sicilian around. Gee! He's getting fat, Shaun.
You couldn't miss him unless you was drunk.'

Shaun said nothing. He had his own plans, and was not
to be rushed.

His wife brought back one piece of information.

'Perelli's got a new man from New York, one of them
Five Points people—Con O'Hara, do you know him?'

Shaun knew him; Mike Feeney knew him better, and had
good reason for disliking him.

'He's a gun, and a slick one—nothing yellow about Con.
He never stops talking, and I guess that means that he'll
just have about time to see the city before he passes on.'

That week Perelli gained another recruit. There was a
man in Boston who was a booze importer and a highly
respected member of the community. Through another
friend he heard of a Harvard boy's misfortune and wrote
to Tony.

*I don't know whether you'll be able to do anything for
this fellow, but he comes of a good family, speaks two or
three languages, and is the kind of man you might find useful.*

So Jimmy McGrath came to Chicago with a letter of
introduction, and a sense of humiliation which was all the
more bitter because it was deserved. He had been expelled
from a great university for a theft which was both mean
and stupid, and which in his sober moments he could not
understand. The college authorities accepted inebriation as
the admission of another and even more serious offence.
It was certainly no excuse. Jimmy scribbled a hurried note
to his New England mother, went into hiding in New

York and, after a futile month spent in searching for work, accepted the rail fare and the letter of introduction which brought him to the Venetian magnificence of Tony Perelli's apartment.

He was tall, tow-headed, good-looking, nervous. Perelli liked him from the start, though he was puzzled as to how he could place him. There were the makings here of a Big Shot. He had a well-ordered mind, and would certainly become a capable organiser. But a Big Shot must be blooded. Here, too, was a substitute for Vinsetti, but again he must qualify. Tony's rule was inflexible: a man must have blood on his hands before he was initiated into the inner mysteries.

It was not his sense of drama but his sense of safety which dictated this condition. A man must be 'in'—up to his neck. There must be no member of the outfit so guilt-less that he could take the stand without fear or knowledge of guilt. You were either in or out.

There was a farm in the country where members of the gang rusticated. It was a sort of club, and it had its own shooting-range. Perelli sent the boy down with Ricardo, champion of all machine-gun choppers.

'Give him the keys,' he instructed, and by 'keys' he meant the freedom of this drab little world.

Ricardo reported a week later that the pupil showed no promise.

'He hasn't the nerve for it,' he said. 'You'd better find him something easier first, Tony.'

So Jimmy McGrath was brought back to Chicago and was 'given the keys' of that territory which Perelli ruled so efficiently. He met gangsters, men on the one side or the other, and a few who were on neither but were in danger from both. For some reason or other he liked Shaun O'Donnell and, more wonderful still, O'Donnell liked him and took him to his apartment off North Place and intro- duced him to his wife.

'One of Perelli's mob, ain't you?' she asked disparagingly. 'Say, why do you go and get yourself fixed up with them Sicilians?'

'Leave the kid alone—that's his trouble,' said Shaun. 'You going to be Tony's fixer, Jimmy?'

Jimmy was puzzled.

'Well, I guess I'm going to be anything that he makes me,' he said.

Shaun looked at him thoughtfully.

'He'll be wanting a fixer now that he's humped off Vinsetti.'

'His best friend—that's the kind of yellow dog he is,' interrupted Mrs. O'Donnell.

Shaun explained.

'Vinsetti ran around and fixed things. He saved Perelli a lot of trouble.'

He might in truth and in justice have said that he himself had been relieved from many an embarrassing situation by the intervention of the fixer.

There was a fourth man at the luncheon, a gloomy Italian who was introduced as Mr. Camona. Exactly what role he played in the complicated business of Shaun's activities Jimmy did not know. The man spoke little and then only in monosyllables. Throughout the meal he ate and drank, and when he was not eating and drinking he stared blankly out of the window and seemed immersed in his thoughts. If he spoke at all it was in very bad English. Later, Perelli was to give the man's history. He was a Sicilian, who had been smuggled into the United States without a passport.

Mike Feeney controlled a number of alky cookers, men and women who distilled denatured alcohol, later to be doctored and bottled and sold to people who could not afford the best, and certainly got as near the worst as made no difference. Camona had been a bandit, had certainly suffered imprisonment in Italy, and was a fugitive from justice when he was imported into Chicago. His job had to do with the organisation of the alky cookers. Incidentally, he had served in the Machine Gun Corps of the Italian Army and was a useful recruit to Mike Feeney's corps of killers.

Either Camona or the driver of the car which carried him was at fault one evening. Tony was driving back from the opera with two of his trusted gang. He had turned into a side street off Michigan Avenue when another car drew level. Tony dropped to the floor as a hail of machine-gun bullets came through the window. One of his companions was not so fortunate, and went down with a bullet through his neck. It was all over in a few seconds. Four alert eyes saw a drooping moustache behind the sights of the machine-gun.

Tony drove the wounded man to hospital and came back to his apartment, very calm and unflurried. Minn Lee, who was waiting up for him, had no idea what had happened, though she supposed it was something serious, for Tony ordered her peremptorily to bed.

Camona lived in a little apartment house on the south side. He arrived home at two o'clock in the morning, was putting his key in the door when a man walked up behind him, laid a pistol against the back of his head, fired, walked back with the greatest unconcern to the waiting car, and was whisked off before the nearest police patrol was within sight.

'Good work, Con.'

Perelli congratulated his newest recruit at breakfast the next morning, and Con O'Hara, stocky, classily tailored and interminably talkative, grinned at the compliment. It was his first solo job for Perelli.

'Clean, Tony—that's my speciality. I never give a guy more than one, and after that his name's "was". I could have got him on the street, but there was a broad saying good night to her feller. I see him go up the stairs and nicked out me thirty-eight ...'

'Sure, sure.'

Tony had little patience with people who dramatised their actions.

'You're a swell feller.'

Jimmy learned the news from the afternoon editions and was shocked. Here was a man with whom he had sat two days earlier—a living, breathing entity, with a history and a future, and who was now nothing but an object of curiosity to certain police officers and a name on a sprawling headline.

'Who do you think did it?' he asked Tony.

'I did it, Jimmy.' Perelli's eyes never left the boy's. 'Sure. That guy tried to stop me last night. He poked a machine-gun on me—the nerve!'

41

'Were you in the car that was fired at?' asked Jimmy incredulously.

He had read of the shooting on Michigan Avenue, but no names had been mentioned.

Perelli nodded.

'Sure.'

'Are you certain it was Camona?' Jimmy was unconvinced.

Tony Perelli laughed softly. He was tickled by the effect of his confession.

'That's the way it is, Jimmy—killing and killing! I don't want to kill nobody, but what are you to do when these guys come after you? There's no law for us, Jimmy: we've got to be our own police and our own executioners. If a guy gives you the works you've got to give it him back, and if he gets you then the other boys have got to see you right. That's the way it goes. Suppose I go to the police, eh, and say: "Mr. Camona poked a machine-gun on me," what do all them lawyers say, Jimmy? "Proof! Where's your proof?" And the only proof I've got is my eyes and something here'—he tapped his chest. 'In this racket one of two things happens: you bump or you're bumped. And you see why, Jimmy. The law's not with us. We can't take a guy before a judge and say, "He's done me dirt," or "He owes me this and he won't pay me," and we can't get injunctions against fellows who come into our territory, and we can't advertise and say, "Our brand of hooch is better than anybody else's." The only law we know is what we get from lawyers and the coppers. A copper don't mean anything after he's on our payroll.'

'Killing a man seems pretty awful—in cold blood.'

Perelli shook his head.

'Killing a guy in hot blood—that's awful, because nine times in ten you make a mistake, and you kill somebody you wouldn't kill, that you didn't oughta kill. Look at the war, Jimmy—I was in that. Killing guys we didn't know—regular fellers, some of them. They'd done nothing wrong, but we just sailed in and killed them and they killed us. There's no sense to it. But when we bump off a man there's a reason, and when we do it it's been worth doing. The

42

things you do in hot blood are generally foolish, and the things you do in cold blood are the worth-while ones.'

So Jimmy had his first lesson in the ethics of gangland and, being young, he was impressed.

'Keep next to Shaun O'Donnell,' Perelli instructed him. 'Maybe you'll be our fixer one of these days.'

McGrath told him of the conversation he had had with Shaun.

'Fine,' said Perelli. 'Him and me thinks alike. Maybe you'll take Victor's place, and that will mean big money for you, Jimmy.'

In his heart of hearts he knew that nobody could take Victor Vinsetti's place. Vinsetti had started steeped in the traditions of this strange underworld, with a complete and exhaustive knowledge of its code, founded on actual contact with its members.

One by one Jimmy met the executive of the gang. Angelo, with his lazy smile and his caustic sense of humour, he liked. The blustering Con O'Hara impressed him less favourably. At last he met Minn Lee. He had heard of her, and was curious to see how far rumour accorded with the truth. Her loveliness swept him off his feet. Whatever natural beauty was hers became enhanced by the setting. Tony spent money lavishly on her. He had imported from the East silks that were worth a little more than their weight in gold. Literally he had changed the tapestry coverings of his furniture to show her colouring to greater advantage. Jimmy came away from that first interview conscious that an empty space in his soul had been filled. He was in love with Minn Lee from the first moment he met her. Thereafter he came very frequently, and Minn Lee watched this development gravely. The one man in the world had come into her life, and that man was Tony Perelli—there could be no other.

Minn Lee looked towards tomorrow, knowing how dread a day that might be. She had inherited from her one European parent a philosophy that went well with the Oriental in her.

Tony asked her one day if she loved him, and she was so long answering that his self-esteem—a very vulnerable point—was made raw.

43

'I suppose so; I think so; yes,' she said. 'Perhaps I don't know what love is. These girls who come in here, they talk about it as though it were a face massage, a new film. I can't talk about it. You frighten me, that's all I know.'

He looked at her, a question in his frown, in the set of his face, in the cold scrutiny of his eyes.

'You love me, huh? Suppose I had a guy waiting in the hall and I said to you, "Minn Lee, go out, he is waiting there with his choppers, and the first one who goes through that door will be killed." Would you ...'

She laughed. Very rarely she laughed, and when she did, it was the low laugh of the European, not the high, shrill giggle that he had heard from Chinese girls.

'I would go, yes, of course.'

His breath came quickly.

'You would be killed, Minn Lee, huh?'

She nodded.

'That's nothing,' she said.

'For anybody else would you do that?'

She thought, her brows puckered.

'No,' she said at last. 'For nobody else.'

A broad smile lightened his fleshy face, his brown eyes sparkled.

'That's love, then, you little fool! You lovely darling!'

He took her in his arms and kissed her for a long time.

4

Tony Perelli thought a lot about his newest recruit. He
liked Jimmy, as far as he was capable of liking anybody
—but he thought too much about him. Jimmy became a
sort of amusing irritation. Always Tony was planning some
place for him in the organisation, and he never seemed to
fit. He hadn't the balance for a fixer, or the knowledge.

He wasn't yellow, but he seemed incapable of murder.
Not that Tony called it murder to dispose of an unfriendly
rival or one who had designs upon his own life.

He seemed to fit into Tony's apartment, was attentive
to Minn Lee, obviously in love with her. Not that Tony
minded that: he regarded it as something of a compliment
that a college boy should approve and confirm his choice.

What could he do? Once or twice he had an inclination
to slip a grand into Jimmy's hand and pack him off by the
20th Century to New York. He could do this, for Jimmy
was not 'in' as a gangster might be counted in. He knew no
secrets, was privy to no more than the confession which
Tony had made as to his responsibility for Vinsetti's death;
and somehow Tony rejected the idea that this boy would
ever give evidence against him even if he were able to do
so.

Kelly was taking an interest in the boy, which was in a
sense unfortunate. The Detective Commissioner was clever;
Tony never underrated his intelligence or his gifts as man-
catcher. Shrewd, cold, remorseless, and yet with a streak
of kindliness which very few people suspected.

He had a trick of calling unexpectedly and usually at the
most awkward moments. He came into Tony's apartment
late one afternoon and saw Minn Lee, not for the first
time. He liked this girl; there was a lot that was fatherly in

Kelly, and he had, too, a sardonic sense of humour that found satisfaction in the knowledge that Minn Lee it was who had lowered herself when she accepted the patronage of the gangster.

'Having a grand time, Minn Lee?' he asked.

Tony grinned.

'Is she having a grand time? Say, that baby started living when she came here.'

'And when does she start dying?' asked Kelly, not taking his eyes off the girl.

Tony frowned. Death—natural death—was a repugnant subject. He, who lived all the time in the shadow of a gun, who knew not from day to day or from hour to hour whence a deadly enemy might spring and a fatal bullet leap, had a horror of illness with possible fatal consequences.

'Ah, 'ow you talk, Chief! Here is life and happiness. Why do you worry my little girl with your talk of death?'

Kelly looked round at him with a crooked smile.

'Worrying you more, I guess,' he said. 'Who's this new kid you've got running around with your hoodlums?'

Tony was ostentatiously puzzled.

'I don't get you . . .'

'You get me all right—McGrath.'

'Oh, Jimmy!' Tony smiled indulgently. 'He's a friend of a friend of mine. He comes from New York.'

'Why couldn't he stay in New York and take a correspondence course in murder?'

Tony shook his head reprovingly.

'An awful word,' he said. 'Murder! There are too many murders in Chicago. Sometimes I wonder if the police are doing their duty, and then I think, "Well, my friend Mr. Kelly is on the job and all will be well, and the hoodlums will be caught and go to the chair." '

'And that makes you sleep comfortable, I guess?' said Kelly, and repeated his question.

'What shall I do with Jimmy? I don't know. He's a good boy, a swell boy. He's no good for rackets—too much of an American gentleman. I guess I'll give him sump'n' to do in Canada.'

'Is he the new fixer?' asked Kelly.

'Fixer?' Tony was blankly bewildered.

'You'll want a new one since you bumped off Vinsetti.' Kelly never minced his words. 'I was wondering who'd take his place.'

Tony Perelli was shocked.

'Since I bumped off Vinsetti, Chief?' His voice was a pained reproach. 'Say, where d'you get that? Vinsetti, my best frien'? No, Chief, it was Mike Feeney's gang got him —I'm giving you the straight of it. That bum Shaun O'Donnell gave him the works.'

'Will you go on to the stand and testify to that?' asked Kelly quickly.

Tony smiled.

'I'm telling you because you, Mr. Kelly, are my frien', not because you, Mr. Kelly, are a cop. I know things but I can prove nothing, and if I could prove something would I be a squealer?'

Kelly knew that trouble was brewing between the rival factions. Perelli's position was growing stronger from day to day. His rivals were being wiped out as effectively as words may be wiped from a slate. Feeney still stood as the most formidable of the gang leaders opposing him, and Feeney meant Shaun O'Donnell.

He tried to get in touch with him, but failed. Making contact with a rival gangster, the inventor of the hand-shake murder, was a little difficult—for had not Tony Perelli on a certain night greeted Emilio Moretti with a firm grip of one hand and shot him with the other?

To Perelli's credit it can be said that he wanted peace. He would pay a big price in cash for harmonious working. He had a sincere distaste for killing. He desired that the war he waged should be fought with the minimum number of casualties, and if money could have brought that happy state of affairs, or any concession other than the loss of territory, he would have bought these conditions at almost any price.

With the little gangs he was ruthless. They kept no faith: took his money one day and muscled in on his joints the day after. For these tiny problems there was only one solution: the little gangsters came and went and none saw their going. Charred bodies were found in the woods; men bound with wire were fished up from the bottom of the river; one was shot dead in the crowded vestibule of a theatre. They had all gone their ways, little dust-heaps, easily flattened—Mike Feeney was a dump of slag, not easily removed.

Third-hand contact could be made with the gang. Jimmy met Shaun O'Donnell and lunched with him. Shaun liked the boy, was secretly amused at his enthusiasms, saw no harm in him, and certainly no danger.

Shaun listened gravely to the boy's naive essay in diplomacy. When Jimmy had finished he shook his head.

'There's nothing to it, kid,' he said. 'Meet Tony! Where —in his gold parlour, the same as Vinsetti did? No, sir!'

'But I swear to you that Tony wants to settle outstanding differences.'

Shaun blinked at this.

'That's a grand way of describing first-degree murder,' he said. 'Sure he wants to settle, and we want to settle too. But we want to do the settling—our guns are as good as his. No, kid, keep out of it. You're a swell guy and you don't properly belong to this racket or any other. And you might tell that bum mick, Con O'Hara, to keep that woman of his away from Tony Perelli. Con's due for the works. We've put a cross on him and he knows it, but all the same, tell him what I told you.'

He looked at Jimmy for a long time.

'Why don't you get out of Chicago, boy?' he asked. 'If it seems good to you, running alongside of a racket, believe me, you're all wrong. Before you know where you are they'll pull you in, and that'll be the end of you. You'd better go home.'

Jimmy shook his head. He was bound now to Chicago by bonds which were not to be broken. Whatever might be his fate, Minn Lee was worth the risk.

He sat for hours in the little room he rented, thinking about her; and in moments of complete sanity marvelled and was shocked at himself that he, with his puritanical upbringing, his ultra-European ideals, should be so completely dominated by a girl who was at best a half-caste, and whose history was, by all his standards, unsavoury.

Yet he could not bring himself to think of her as anything but as he saw her, and as from day to day and from hour to hour she impressed him.

It was a puzzling, baffling sort of existence, this gang life. There were so many ramifications to Tony Perelli's business, so many complexities. Interest overlapped interest; men he had regarded as being henchmen of Perelli, and whom he had never thought of as being anything but loyal adherents to the big man, were, he was to discover, allied to other groups, and their allegiance to Tony the most temporary of associations.

Perelli had partners in specific enterprises, gave those partners protection and shared their gains, and when the enterprise was finished, so, too, was the alliance; and the men with whom you hobnobbed and dined and wined would be waiting to drop you when opportunity offered.

The regulars of the gang, the Angelos and Molos, knew of this arrangement, but Jimmy accepted these alliances as permanent.

There was a nice Italian boy called Salvini, whom he frequently met at Tony Perelli's apartment. He played the violin rather well: Tony had been ecstatic about the quality of his art. Then he had ceased to come, and when Jimmy enquired, both Angelo and Perelli answered vaguely that the work was finished. What the work was Jimmy did not ask. One day he was driving on the Burnham road and saw a crowd gathered around a small sedan. A squad car came howling and jangling past and pulled to a stop behind the stationary machine, scattering the crowd in all directions. Jimmy also pulled up and went forward through the crowd. He arrived as the police lifted an inanimate figure.

The face was terrible to see, yet Jimmy recognised Salvini and almost fainted with horror.

He hurried back to the big apartment and found Tony choosing presents for a party he was giving that night. As soon as they were alone he blurted out the news Perelli listened without comment, unmoved; there was nothing remarkable in that. When Jimmy had finished he nodded.

'Sure it was Salvini,' he said, 'and his own car, Jimmy. That's how it goes. That guy hadn't got the sense to stay quiet. And I spoke to him, Jimmy—I took all that trouble.

49

I said: "Salvini, when this racket is finished maybe I'll bring you into my organisation, but not yet." And what did he do? He went shooting his mouth over Chicago about my business and the Federal officers raided one of my breweries, and it cost me twenty grand to get it open again.'

Jimmy looked at him terrified.

'But you—you!' he gasped. 'Wasn't he one of your men?'

Tony shook his head.

'You—you didn't . . . ?'

Perelli shook his head again.

'Not me, Jimmy. I don't do such things. But I guess one of the boys got sore with him, and that's all there is to it. What could we do—bring a suit in the courts to stop him talking? Wouldn't Chicago laugh if I put the bulls on him? No, Jimmy, that happened just right. There's nothing to it.'

He dismissed the murder airily.

Yet there was a definite line between the gangs. Mike Feeney's executive was on one side, Perelli's on the other. Certain definite territories that might not be invaded, certain no-man's-lands where unceasing battle went on for the possession of this or that strategical point.

Perelli had a monopoly of slot machines—gambling devices which produced a huge profit. Sometimes they would be raided, torn from their place and thrown, broken and smashed, into the street; and after that, dark-faced little men would wander with apparent aimlessness, looking for somebody and conscious that they were being looked for. The end would come with three staccato reports, later the howl of a squad car, the flashing by of an ambulance, and a dishevelled man sitting in Kelly's private room undergoing a grilling.

There was no lack of droppers. You could buy them at a price from New York, Detroit, St. Louis or Philadelphia; expert, two-handed gunmen, who shot with deadly accuracy and never lost their heads in the presence of a pursuing crowd.

Tony seemed to have the pick of them, but his agents watched with unceasing vigilance lest a better man were recruited by the other side—and woe to the recruit!

The business side of the organisation was amazing. They

had laboratories, where spirit was tested by expert ana-
lysts. Liquor came by car and ship and train and even by
plane. The actual trading side of the organisation was so
complicated that only an expert accountant could have
kept track of it.

One day, when Jimmy was having tea at the most fashionable hotel in Chicago, he was hailed by a strident voice, and
Con O'Hara came towards him, beaming. A noisy man,
this Con O'Hara, bursting with confidence; something of
a brute, a boaster, though he had with it all a sense of humour which came in rare flashes.

'Meet Mrs. O'Hara, Jimmy.'

Jimmy looked at the girl and gasped. He had seen her
following O'Hara, but had imagined she was on her way
up to her room. Never did he dream of connecting her
with the stout, uncouth killer. She was fair, tall and slim;
she had the face of a Madonna; the clear grey eyes of a
child, red lips that needed no artificial aid. . . .

'Glad to know you, Mr. McGrath—I've heard a whole
lot about you.'

He wished she hadn't spoken: that lazy, vulgar voice of
hers sounded incongruous.

'Sit down, baby.' O'Hara pulled out a chair. 'We're going
round to the stores, and Maria's going to make a grand
look like two cents.'

He beamed at her, was obviously in love with the girl
whom he called, without any especial authority, Mrs.
O'Hara.

'You said you were going to take me up to see Mr.
Perelli.'

Her pout was theatrical—baby stuff, thought the dis-
illusioned Jimmy.

'Sure I'll take you, but Tony's out this evening. She's
crazy to meet him,' he explained to Jimmy.

'I'd like to meet Mrs. Perelli—the Chinese girl.'

Con's nose wrinkled.

'She's noth'n', kid, just a little Chink. Pretty? Well, maybe she's that, but she's not my idea of pretty.'

She was looking with a steady, appraising eye at Jimmy,
and he knew that she approved without being particularly
interested in him. She liked Chicago, but not quite so much

51

as New York. It was a grand city, but when all her friends were in Brooklyn—well, one felt lonesome.

She must have heard a great deal about Jimmy from Con, for she paid him none of the respect that might be due if she had imagined he held an important position in the organisation. She didn't pity him, either, because Maria Pouluski had not experienced that emotion.

Walking out of the hotel, Jimmy came, most unexpectedly and surprisingly, upon Tony Perelli. He was walking towards Michigan Boulevard and he had his four killers with him, two in front and two behind, and Jimmy suspected there were another four on the opposite sidewalk. Though he was not aware of the fact, Perelli very frequently made these excursions on foot, sometimes to transact a little business of the most trivial character, sometimes to buy presents for Minn Lee, but always to obtain the exercise which he found necessary.

Jimmy had learned enough of Perelli's likes and dislikes not to overtake him. He followed the great man at a respectful distance. They turned right into the Boulevard, and Jimmy noticed that the four guards closed on their leader. They had not gone more than fifty yards when a closed car, driving near the kerb, slowed just ahead of the party. . . .

The reports were deafening. A machine-gun bullet ricochetted so close to Jimmy's face that the 'wham' of it almost hurt him. One of the guards was on the pavement. Three others were shooting two-handed at the car, which made a sudden swerve and came to a halt in the centre of the road.

The fast-moving traffic stopped or dodged in time. There was a scurry of policemen; one leaped on to the running-board and pulled out the youth who was driving. He was dazed; blood was streaming down the back of his ear; his face was the colour of chalk.

The other two men were huddled on the back seat of the car. Tony's gunmen were experts.

Tony came back from police headquarters a very angry man, and it was unusual for him to display temper. One of his best droppers had been killed, and the fact that two of the attackers were now lying under tarpaulins, awaiting identification, was no satisfaction to him.

'They were Feeney's men all right. Shaun O'Donnell—yeah?'

Minn Lee was putting iodine very tenderly on a scarred knuckle.

'That's how it goes, Jimmy,' he said more quietly. 'This morning Shaun sent a message to me asking for a little peace talk. This afternoon he sent his torpedoes to make me more peaceful, eh? And he's been speaking against Minn Lee very badly. Oh, Jimmy, the things he said about Minn Lee!'

Jimmy stared at him.

'Why?' he asked hotly. 'Minn Lee's done no harm to him.'

'That's how it goes, Jimmy.' Perelli nodded. 'Presently I'll have a talk with you.'

'Presently' was very soon. He led Jimmy out to the balcony that overlooked Chicago in the glory of a gorgeous Italian sunset.

'You will see O'Donnell, Jimmy. I think he will come if you telephone.'

'But what can I do . . .' began Jimmy.

Tony silenced him with a gesture.

'Say you want to fix things. You want to ask him how far he'll go. You can get him on the telephone and say you want to make everything right with me, but that I don't know you're phoning. I don't want any trouble, Jimmy, and you're the guy that can fix everything.'

Shaun O'Donnell was a most difficult man to meet. There was none more slippery, more shy of company and the unprotected streets. Though Jimmy McGrath was not aware of the fact, he had seen more of Mike Feeney's aid than any man in gangland.

It took him two hours to reach O'Donnell by phone and his reception was not encouraging.

'If it was anybody but you, Jimmy, I'd tell 'em to go plumb to hell,' he said. 'He's making you a fixer, eh? Why, last week he was telling the world you were dumb.'

'Couldn't we meet somewhere?' asked Jimmy.

There was a silence.

'Perelli doesn't think I had anything to do with that shooting today, does he, Jimmy?'

53

There was an unusual note of anxiety in Shaun O'Donnell's voice.

'Why . . . yes.' Jimmy hesitated. 'I guess he does, Shaun.'

The very honesty of the answer took Shaun O'Donnell off his guard.

'O.K. I'll meet you. Come along to the corner of Atlantic and 95th at ten o'clock tonight. Bring nobody with you, Jimmy—I'm trusting you. I don't think anything will come of it.'

Jimmy duly reported the result of the talk and Tony clapped him on the back.

'Jimmy, you're swell,' he said. 'You go along in your little sedan, get out and wait on the corner till Shaun comes. Con can sit on the floor of the car where he can't be seen. And maybe you won't want Con.'

Jimmy listened, his head in a whirl.

'How's that?' he asked dully. 'What do you want me to do?'

Perelli's eye was cold and glittering. He took from his pocket a neat little Colt, passed it, butt foremost, to Jimmy.

'Stick it under your armpit, Jimmy, and give him the works—good and plenty.'

There was a complete silence. Jimmy's face was white.

'What do you want me to do?'

It did not sound like his own voice.

'It isn't what I want you to do, it's what I'm telling you to do,' said Perelli steadily. 'You're going to bump off Shaun O'Donnell.'

Jimmy McGrath found himself unlocking the door of his room without realising how he came to be there. He was moving mechanically, thinking not at all. The world had become a monstrous unreality; the living people who thronged the streets and occupied the wild tangle of motor traffic, that moved and stopped obediently at the green and red traffic lights, were of another kind to himself. They had homes and relatives and interests. Thousands of them were dressing for dinner at this moment; millions were relaxing in the security of their apartments and houses, having no worries beyond the domestic problems which beset every household. . . .

He belonged to a people apart. They were human beings; he was something entirely different, a potential murderer, the cold-blooded assassin of a man who had trusted him, and probably had never trusted another. Well, he must get over that. Jimmy showed his teeth in a painful grin.

Shaun O'Donnell trusted him, and he was going to shoot him. He couldn't believe it. He wrote the words down on a sheet of paper: 'Shaun O'Donnell trusts me, and I'm going to murder him', and even then he could not find the reality of this bizarre situation. He tore the paper into little pieces and, dropping them piece by piece through a blazing gas-ring, saw them fall, pitiful, charred morsels, on the enamelled cover below. That was how he was going into the fire—white, comparatively, and that was how he was coming out—the charred, ugly embers of a man.

That he might be killed himself did not concern him. He sat with his head in his hands, thinking it over and over; had wild ideas of warning Shaun. It was simple. A lift of the telephone, a number—and then what? Tony Perelli would know all about it. News of that kind travels like an electric spark throughout the underworld. The big secrets on which the police speculate are no secrets below ground. Of course Perelli would know that he had been betrayed, and there was only one punishment for that.

Yet it was not the fear of punishment which held Jimmy back: it was a perverse sense of loyalty to a man he liked, to the new clan he had joined, which revolted him, yet demanded his implicit obedience.

This was the end of it, then—the end of Jimmy McGrath. If he killed Shaun O'Donnell, the Feeney gang would put the cross on him. He would be marked for death—he laughed at the thought. No fear here, either. If he killed Shaun he deserved death: that was the beginning and the end of it. Tony would give him protection, would send him out of Chicago till some grander crime, directed against the Feeney crowd, wiped out all memory of lesser offences.

He was desperately sorry for Shaun but, for some curious reason, not particularly sorry for Mrs. O'Donnell, who had treated him so well and civilly. Somehow he did not think of her as a dependent woman; he could imagine in her none of the romance and tragedy of widowhood. He

thought of her only as a cog in the machinery of Mike
Feeney's organisation. You might fear her but not be afraid
of her.

There came a knock at his door, and he jumped out of
his chair. He went out into the little hall and opened the
door. Con O'Hara was there; he was dressed in a new grey
suit, a hard felt hat was on the back of his head, and in his
large face was struck a fragrant cigar.

'Busy, kid?' he asked.

Jimmy opened the door wider and invited him in with
a gesture.

'Livin' alone, eh? Say, these apartment houses ain't fit for
a dorg! Tony talks about putting you into a swell apartment.'

He looked round the gaunt room disapprovingly.

'Not fit for a dorg!' he repeated.

And then he sat down at the table opposite Jimmy, looking at the boy with half-closed eyes.

'All set for tonight, kid?'

Jimmy shrugged. He wanted to appear unconcerned,
called upon all his reserve of vanity to aid him in this affec-
tation of indifference.

'Sure.'

'You come round to the garage and take my flivver, and
don't pull a rod on the man you'll find sitting down on the
floor, because that'll be me. Feeney's crowd are Big Eyes.
They'll be watching the car go out, and if I'm sitting there
with you they'll know all about it. The first thing that'll
happen to us will be a roadster coming alongside, and a
typewriter working double time!'

Con O'Hara was a shrewd, understanding man. To give
this loud-mouthed braggart his full measure of credit, he
was absolutely without fear. He had been a dropper since
his boyhood, had killed his man in his teens. Tonight's work
meant nothing unusual; nothing at any rate to stir his pulses
in anticipation.

He had met Jimmy's type before: had superintended
the blooding of many boys, had seen them swagger to their
villainy and cringe, found them white and black and occa-
sionally yellow. There was nothing yet to suggest that
Jimmy was yellow. All these preliminary pallors and tremb-
lings and breathlessness were inevitable to the occasion.

'Say, don't let it worry you, Jimmy.' He took out his cigar and blew a cloud of smoke to the dingy ceiling. 'Why, it's noth'n'. Everybody's got to die sometime, ain't they? Say, to read them God-awful newspapers, you'd think that if a guy hadn't been bumped off he'd have lived for ever! Ain't that the fact? Did you ever think, Jimmy, what you may be savin' a feller by putting him out? All the sickness an' the pain an' everythin'!'

Jimmy made a gesture of impatience.

'I don't want to think about it—that's the truth.'

'Of course you don't want to think about it,' soothed Con.

He gave some instructions, dictated a short timetable, and swaggered out to report to his superior the result of his visit.

Tony was not at home; he and Minn Lee were driving somewhere in the country. Perelli often drove out in his armoured car for no other reason than for a little recreation. He had no set times, no regular routes. After several attempts to ambuscade him Feeney had given up hope of writing finish to the feud through this method.

Angelo, as usual, was in the apartment, checking documents that had come from Canada. Angelo Verona was something more than confidential clerk to Tony Perelli. By all he was regarded as the legitimate successor to the leadership of the gang. Oddly enough, he was not a Sicilian. What his real name was nobody quite knew; they accepted Verona both to identify him and to establish his birthplace. He was clever, combining strategical sense with considerable business ability.

The Feeneys and the O'Donnells of life respected and feared him. Shaun used to say that he was the most dangerous member of the Perelli crowd. Angelo was a brilliant two-handed gunman, a machine-gun expert, and an authority on alcohol. As a rule he took little part in the outside fighting, confining himself to, and taking part in, all that happened within the orbit of Tony Perelli's personal leadership.

If Shaun O'Donnell spoke of him in complimentary terms, Angelo had no respect at all for O'Donnell. He did not like Irishmen. He liked Con O'Hara less than any Irishman he had ever met.

'Is the chief around?' asked Con, finding the most comfortable chair in the apartment and dropping into it, as he

57

produced another cigar and bit off the end.

Angelo looked up from his work.

'He does not like you to call him "chief", Con,' he said quietly.

He had the quick, staccato speech of a man who is conscious of speaking a foreign language and is anxious to get every sentence pronounced as quickly and as correctly as possible. Yet Angelo had been born in America and, except for the brief domestic period of his life, had spoken no other language.

'I've seen the kid,' said Con.

Angelo, busy with an account, grunted something.

'That boy will never make a dropper in a million years, Angelo.'

'Is that so?' Angelo was politely interested. 'The kid being . . . ?'

'Jimmy McGrath. But Tony needn't worry about to-night. Say, I'll handle Shaun . . .'

Angelo leaned back in his chair, and his thin smile was offensive.

'I surely get all the news from you, Con,' he said. 'What's all this stuff about Shaun? Say, you ought to be a newspaper man! Why don't you go down to the *Tribune* office and give them the dope on it?'

Con's frown was heavy and black.

'I suppose I can't talk with you, huh? What's the matter with all you guys, Angelo, pretending there's nothin' doin' when there's sump'n' doing?'

Angelo's dark eyes transfixed him.

'There's nothin' doing in this outfit that's worth talking about,' he said emphatically. 'I was reading in a book somewhere that the best thing about a torpedo was that it made no noise, and that's a pretty good kind of torpedo. Maybe in New York people like to hear themselves talk, but around here, Con, we behave as though there was a mike in every corner of the room, all leading down to police headquarters.'

Con's lips curled.

'Police headquarters! Listen, you fellers . . .'

'Us fellers know them fellers,' said Angelo, emphasising every word.

Tony came in at that moment, alone. Minn Lee had gone to her room. He nodded lazily to Con and, walking over to where Angelo was sitting, talked to him in a low voice and in Italian. Tony often chose that language for his more confidential communications, and these were the only occasions when Angelo responded in his mother tongue.

It was a practice which irritated Con. It made him feel out of things.

'Say, what's the idea of leavin' me out of it?'

Perelli turned his insolent gaze on his servant.

'Did anybody tell you you were in it, Mr. Con O'Hara?' he asked.

'Well, I happen to be here . . .' began Con.

'And who invited you here? Maybe you think this is a speakeasy where you can drop in just as and when, Con?'

'I come in to tell you about Jimmy,' said Con, his vanity hurt. 'Say, I'd rather do that job without Jimmy. That kid looks like falling apart.'

Perelli walked slowly towards the man, standing before him, his hands on his hips, his head tilted on one side.

'Did I ask you anything about what you'd rather do?' he demanded. 'This is Jimmy's killing. If he gets this fellow without your gun, let him get him. You're there to help Jimmy, in case he gets nervous and Shaun pulls on him. It isn't a question of taking him—he's taking you along. Get that, Con O'Hara.'

Con's face was dark and sulky. He was an injured man.

'That's O.K.,' he grumbled.

He tried to find an excuse for remaining and producing an atmosphere less hostile; and failing, went forth ignominiously in silence.

For a long time after he had gone neither of the two men spoke, and then:

'It is wrong to send that boy, Antonio,' said Angelo in Italian. 'If you wish to give him experience, let him try a job less important.'

Tony shook his head.

'He's not "in" yet,' he said. 'That's the only way to get him there. Till Jimmy's got to watch every step, till he knows that every one of Mike Feeney's gunmen is looking and waiting for him, he just won't know what this racket is.'

Angelo shook his head.

'I disagree. We'll let it stay at that,' he said. 'You're going to break a good workman.'

Tony did a lot of city travel. He had depots and offices, laboratories, breweries, and places less easy to write about, that required his occasional personal attention, and since there were many of them, hardly a day passed when he did not leave his apartment. Usually the hours between six and nine were the dullest of the day for Minn Lee, and the arrival of Jimmy had brought her an appreciable relief from the tedium of the early evening.

Jimmy's visits to the apartment had been fewer lately. She liked Jimmy, in a sense was fond of him. He stood for something entirely outside any experience she had had since she had left college. He and Commissioner Kelly stood for an America with which she was no longer brought into actual contact. When Kiki, the Japanese servant, came to her room to tell her that Jimmy was waiting in the salon, she felt a little lightening of the heart and, putting down the embroidery on which she was working, she hurried out to meet him.

'Why, Jimmy, I thought you were never coming again . . .' she began, and then she saw his face.

It was white and set. There was a new coldness in his eyes.

'Aren't you well, Jimmy?'

He shook his head.

'I'm O.K., Minn Lee. Thought I'd call in and have a little talk with you.'

She smiled and indicated a chair.

'A long talk, Jimmy,' she said. 'Tony will not be home until ten o'clock.'

He drew a long breath. By ten o'clock many things would have happened, the whole course of his life changed.

He found it difficult to begin, but at last stumbled into an opening.

'If anything happens to me, Minn Lee . . . I want you to know that you've made a whole lot of difference. . . . You've been something terribly big in my life, Minn Lee . . . that sounds mushy and insincere, but it's God's truth. I guess folks would think I'm crazy to feel about you like I do. I know such a lot about you and about Perelli. . . . You're not married, are you?'

She shook her head.

'Why, of course, I knew that,' he went on, 'but it doesn't matter. I couldn't give you anything. I'm just a poor, weak, amateur hoodlum.'

He laughed bitterly.

'I guess I'm being sorry for myself.'

There was a silence here.

'What do you mean—if anything happens to you, Jimmy?' she asked quietly, and he forced a smile.

'Well, you know what this racket is,' he said. 'Here today —and gone tomorrow.'

'Why should you be gone tomorrow, Jimmy?' Her grave eyes did not leave his face. 'Is something terrible happening tonight?'

He opened his mouth to reply, changed his mind and shook his head.

'No. That's all, Minn Lee.'

He rose abruptly to his feet.

'Are you going?' she asked, in surprise.

He nodded. He had found it sufficiently difficult to control his voice; it was almost impossible now. He walked swiftly towards her, took one of her hands in his and for a moment fondled it before he pressed it to his lips. In another instant he was gone.

The garage was only a few blocks away; he went there on foot, asking for Con's car, but not in Con O'Hara's name. For garage purposes Con O'Hara had a distinct name. One of the hands pointed out the vehicle and took no further notice.

His heart was beating painfully as he walked up to the passenger door and pulled it open.

'The other door, you bonehead!' hissed a voice, and he saw the figure of Con O'Hara crouching on the floor, and over his bent head a black cloth.

He slammed the door closed, walked round the car and got in behind the steering-wheel. It was very dark; the main road was wet and slippery. He drew out of the garage, turned left and moved at a leisurely pace, coming to Michigan Boulevard in five minutes.

A car passed him. Somebody switched a spotlight full in his face. He was momentarily blinded.

'What did I tell you, Jimmy?'

Con O'Hara removed the cloth which covered him.

'They were looking for me.'

'Why you?' asked Jimmy. It was the first rational question he had asked the man.

'Me or anybody,' said the other impatiently. 'If I'd been sitting up there by your side, do you know what would have happened? They'd have poked a machine-gun on to us, and that would have been farewell Chicago.'

They reached the outskirts of the city and were to undergo another test. A second car came slowly towards them, a light struck Jimmy right in the face and held. He ducked his head to avoid the glare, passed out of the circle of light, blinded.

'That's Shaun,' said Con in a low voice. 'Mike Feeney doesn't know he's meeting you, or we wouldn't have gone far, believe me, kid! Take your time, Jimmy—you've got all of it!'

They came at last to the rendezvous, a deserted little boulevard, from which ran at right angles a street filled with middle-class houses. The corner block was unbuilt on, and was surrounded by a plain fence. Jimmy drew the car to the sidewalk. His heart was thumping so madly now that he could hardly breathe. He put his hand into his pocket; the gun was there, and he thumbed back the hammer and, drawing out the weapon, laid it on the seat by his side.

There was nobody in sight, except a car or two that went whizzing townwards.

Would Shaun come by car? If he did there would be trouble. Jimmy hoped he would come that way, attended by gunmen, with a machine-gun and every form of frightfulness to wipe out the monstrous affront of his murder.

Whatever happened, Shaun must be killed. Though it break his heart to do this, the enemy of Perelli must be blotted out of existence.

'Can you see anything, kid?' Con's muffled voice came up from the floor.

'Nothing.'

He looked through the rear window. A woman was walking along towards them; she carried a heavy basket. She was obviously a help at one of the houses. She passed; and then Jimmy saw a figure walking quickly towards them along the sidewalk, keeping in the shadows. Nearer and nearer it came, and the boy almost collapsed when he recognised the man.

He stepped out of the car, his legs giving beneath him, his hand gripping the gun which he held behind him.

'Is that you, Jimmy?'

Shaun O'Donnell came quickly towards him.

'Listen, kid: I can only give you a few minutes. There's trouble in town, and . . .'

Jimmy tried to steady his gun. He jerked it in front of him and fired. The first shot missed. He fired again. Shaun O'Donnell was reaching for his revolver, staggered back against the fence.

'You . . . !'

Three shots thundered in rapid succession almost in Jimmy's ear. Con O'Hara fired coolly, scientifically, unerringly. Shaun O'Donnell slumped down by the fence. Somewhere a whistle blew.

'Beat it!' snarled Con, and leapt for the car.

He took the wheel. Jimmy sat beside him, a huddled figure, incapable of movement or thought.

Shaun O'Donnell was dead . . . he had killed him . . . lured him to his death . . . the blackest of treachery . . . .

'Oh, my God!'

The car was flying. Con O'Hara had once been a racing motorist and his vehicle was tuned for speed.

As he drove, he talked.

'I got him. Kid, you missed him. Say, you fell apart. I'm not blaming you, Jimmy. You ain't got my experience, nor my nerve either. Don't worry, kid. Sit tight and take a drink of that stuff you'll find in the pocket. Say, did you see him drop? First shot. That baby was right under the heart, Jimmy. Say, when I pull a rod on a man, that man don't take no interest in noth'n' but dying.'

Jimmy sat, staring through the smeared glass of the window. Murderer . . . Jimmy McGrath, murderer!

5

The news flashed through Chicago—Shaun O'Donnell had got his. And it was news of the first importance, for Shaun was a Big Shot amongst little shots; a power; a man to whom lesser gangsters turned, if not for comfort, for very material assistance. A Big Shot in this sense, that at his word men died quickly and often in painful circumstances.

It was Shaun who had taken Perelli's boyhood friend so daringly that it was the talk of their world. Perelli and this man, whose name was Amigo, had been sitting together in the latter's apartment, and the host had been called out to a telephone call. He was never seen again till they found him in a thin plantation near the Burnham Road, nor easily recognisable, for he had been shot and buried in quicklime. Tony remembered that till it was convenient to forget: friendships must not interfere with business.

And here was Shaun dead, and his wife displaying an unexpected aspect of femininity in a fit of hysterics, crying and screaming blue murder, and Detective Harrigan's car at the door, waiting to take her to the Brother's Hospital, where Shaun lay beyond any other help than that which the hastily summoned priest could give to him.

The little priest stood with Harrigan by the bedside of the unconscious man. The mud-stained motorcyclist patrol who had found the body was an interested spectator. Curiously enough, in all his years of service, he had never been brought face to face with a gang shooting.

The intern, white-coated, cool, very capable, a little indifferent, conscious only that he was to be relieved at midnight and had a date with a girl at the Blackstone, where the Medical Association were having their dance, could afford to wait with patience for the inevitable end.

Harrigan, the first to hear the news, had certain futile duties to perform, and their futility was emphasised by the whispered question of the priest.

'Have you any idea who did this?'

The intern heard the whisper and looked round, smiled and nodded.

'You needn't whisper, talk just as loud as you like: you're not disturbing him, because he can't hear you. He'll be conscious again, but not for long, I guess.'

The priest drew a long breath. He, too, was meeting this form of dissolution for the first time. He was young, Rome-trained, an idealist and new to Chicago. His ideals were only capable of attainment given certain reactions in his flock—those reactions were neither audible nor visible. He spoke English with a slight accent; some day was to go back to Rome and the tranquillity of a bishopric, for he was of noble birth, expensively educated and marked for advancement.

'These crimes, I cannot understand them!' He was puzzled. 'Every week I read in the newspapers of some-body who is killed this way. It is dreadful! This is a gang shooting?'

Harrigan nodded slowly.

'Yeh. He was one of Mike Feeney's crowd.'

The priest looked at the dying man.

'I met him. Father Romani introduced him. Shaun O'Donnell? Of course, he was an altar boy at the Holy Name Cathedral.'

'That's so,' said Harrigan.

A curious fatality pursued these boys who had started so promisingly in the cloistered quiet of the great cathedral.

'Where did you find him?' asked Harrigan, addressing the interested policeman, who woke up with a start.

He had found him on the corner of Atlantic and 95th. He himself was two blocks away when the shooting started and had come up in time to see the sedan melt into the darkness. He had run to the nearest phone and got on to headquarters.

'He said nothing?' asked Harrigan.

The policeman thought he had said 'Jimmy'. He was certain he had cursed a little 'in a kinda drowsy way'.

Harrigan thought it was a queer place for a bumping and wondered how Shaun had come to be there without his guard and his killers, why he had stopped his own car two hundred yards down the road, and had driven out in Chicago without a single attendant. He frowned as he considered all the possibilities of the case, and wondered aloud if Mike Feeney had put him on the spot.

It seemed a new phrase for the priest.

'Put him on the spot?'

'Sure, Father,' nodded Harrigan, and then the priest remembered that he had heard of such fatalities.

'Sent to his death by his own gang? Horrible! But why?'

Harrigan shook his head again and answered patiently.

'Sometimes it's the price they pay for peace,' he said. 'Gang leaders can't always control their own men, and if one of them starts to shoot up a rival gang, the leader can either take on his quarrel or put him on the spot—send him to some place where the other gang can get him.'

The young priest whispered:

'A human sacrifice!'

'It would be, Father,' said Harrigan, with a frosty smile, 'if they were human, but these . . .' His gesture towards the bed was very expressive.

Shaun was moving. They could hear the faint sound of his voice. The intern looked up quickly and beckoned with a jerk of his head—his hands being occupied.

'You won't have much time,' he said in a low voice.

Harrigan sat down on the side of the bed and bent over.

'Hullo, Shaun. You know me, boy? Pat Harrigan. Captain Pat Harrigan . . .'

He saw a gleam of intelligence in the tired eyes.

'You're all jake, boy! I've been a good friend of yours, Shaun. . . . Sure I have. Looked after your mother the first time you went to stir, didn't I? You're going to tell me who did this, aren't you?'

A whisper from the wreck on the bed. Harrigan bent his ear and nodded.

'Sure, I've sent for your wife. I rushed my own car for her. They never gave you a chance, Shaun. They put you on the spot, didn't they?' He paused expectantly.

Shaun O'Donnell understood, but there was no answer.

66

'Come clean with it, kid. It wasn't Feeney? Two of the Perelli gang, wasn't it, Shaun?'

The eyes were fixed in a stare, and Harrigan's voice became more urgent.

'You're not going to God with a lie on your lips, are you? Wasn't it Con O'Hara bumped you? Shaun, for God's sake, don't go out without tellin' the truth! Perelli's gang got you? Con O'Hara, wasn't it?'

He waited, waited. . . .

True to the gang tradition, Shaun did not speak. The police meant nothing. Their promise of vengeance meant nothing. He was silent not because he did not trust the police, not from any mistaken sense of honour. He had no faith in policemen, because he knew that his own police would settle all accounts and his own executioners would move expeditiously and unerringly to avenge him. He relied on a higher authority than the authority of the established law. In his dimming consciousness he knew that the machinery of revenge would be working, and working swiftly.

Harrigan read the signs in the eyes. He turned to the priest and beckoned him forward.

'That's how they are—dumb!' he said bitterly, and knelt, looking at his watch as he did so. Shaun did not keep him waiting very long.

Mrs. O'Donnell came too late to the hospital to do any more than make preparations for her husband's funeral. If she had wept she did not weep now. Her instructions were practical to the point of heartlessness. It may have been that this gruesome business of designating the exact quality of silver casket that should receive all that was mortal of Shaun O'Donnell, and the injunction that it should cost no more than so much, were an anodyne to the stark desolation of her soul.

The intern, dressed for his party, listened, amazed, to the discussion that took place in his office. She had with her three of Mike Feeney's most trusted chiefs and an effeminate youth who wrote shorthand in a book with a red leather cover with gold edging. She left the hospital with the three men and drove back to her apartment with them.

The most important of these, 'Spike' Mulligan, weedy-looking, hatchet-faced, sandy-haired, with the appearance of a well-furnished bank clerk, by nature more deadly than a ring snake, turned to the more pressing business of reprisal. Mike Feeney was in Indiana, superintending certain important negotiations. Mulligan had got him on the telephone and Mike was speeding back through the night.

'It was Jimmy McGrath and Con O'Hara,' said Mrs. O'Donnell. 'You saw them coming back, didn't you, Spike?'

Spike nodded.

'I knew Shaun was going to see Jimmy,' she went on. 'He didn't often tell me where he was going, but he told me that, and I tried to get him to stay home. Perelli sent Jimmy because he knew Shaun trusted him. Those two men have got to be fixed before Mike gets back.'

'That's what I say,' said Spike.

The other men nodded.

'Jimmy's nothing—just yeller ...'

'But he ain't going to get away with it,' said Spike. 'O'Hara's got an apartment on North State. He's living there with his woman.'

'But Perelli ...' said one of the others.

'Ain't one of you boys got enough guts to get him?' Mrs. O'Donnell spat the question.

Spike looked thoughtfully at his well-manicured fingernails.

'That's not easy, Mrs. O'Donnell.' There was a note of apology in his tone. 'The other two, why, they don't think that anybody's seen them—they'll be easy. I'll get Con and Jimmy if they're not on the run.'

The woman's hard face set into an ugly mask of hate.

'I'd fix Perelli if he'd see me,' she said between her teeth.

There was a long, long silence, and then she rose abruptly from the table.

'Go and get these boys,' she said, and the 'droppers' went out to their mission.

The reactions of Jimmy McGrath were peculiar and unexpected. He was quite cool, his mind perfectly ordered, when he said good night to Con O'Hara and walked the rest of the way home.

He had taken his step and there was nothing else for him to do but to wait. He was beyond pity either for Shaun O'Donnell or for himself. There was blood on his hands— the blood of a friend. He was a cold-hearted midnight assassin. He had not understood these shootings till now. They had been beyond his comprehension. He had never been able to put himself in the place of the killer, and now he was a killer himself. He was numb to grief or remorse. It was as though a local anaesthetic had been applied to his sense of right and wrong. Just numb. The more sensitive places of his mind were beyond feeling.

He went upstairs to his room, unlocked the door, put on a light, bolted the door behind him and washed his hands. He was terribly thirsty, drank glass after glass of water. He took off his coat and vest, loosened his collar and, kicking off his shoes, lay down on the bed, pulling the coverlet over him, and switched out the light.

Sleep should have been denied him, yet he slept immediately, and was heavy in dreamless oblivion when a tap came to his door. He was awake instantly and off the bed. His gun was on the table where he had left it. He took it up, his heart thumping painfully. Again came the knock, and then a voice he recognised—it was Angelo's.

'Open the door, Jimmy.'

He drew back the bolts and Angelo came in.

'Sleeping, eh?' He was frankly surprised. 'Put on your shoes and coat.'

'Does Tony want me?'

Angelo shook his head slightly.

'He doesn't want to see you, but we've got another place for you to sleep tonight. This one ain't so good, Jimmy.'

Jimmy McGrath felt his throat go dry.

'Do they know . . .' he stammered, 'about Shaun and— and me . . . ?'

'Sure they know,' said Angelo, coolly. 'Con was seen driving back to town with you.'

Angelo looked at his watch.

'Step on it,' he said curtly.

Jimmy fumbled his feet into his shoes, drew on his coat and, slipping his gun into his pocket, followed the other man out of the room.

'Put out the light and lock the door,' commanded Angelo, and Jimmy obeyed the first instruction.

He was trembling violently. His breath came in short, shallow gasps. He felt like a man who had been running for a long distance.

They went downstairs into the street. A little way along a car was drawn up and loitering on the sidewalk were two men. He did not speak to them, nor did Angelo. They left them behind.

A quarter of an hour later Jimmy found a new lodging in a small hotel near to Tony Perelli's apartment.

'Don't open the door to anybody. I'll send somebody early in the morning and then you can have breakfast brought in. Tony will want to see you.'

'Where's Con?'

'Home,' said Angelo impatiently.

He was not in the mood to answer questions, had himself been pulled out of bed to secure the new recruit to the murder squad, and was anxious to return to that comfortable place.

He waited outside the door until he heard the bolt snap home, and went down in the elevator.

Perelli owned this hotel and Jimmy was safe for the night.

Spike Mulligan did not go immediately in search of Jimmy McGrath. He accepted the harder task first. Con O'Hara's apartment was located. There was a light in the window and it was to be seen from the street. Spike went to the nearest drug store and called him on the phone.

'Say, is that you, Con?'

Mulligan knew O'Hara—they had been members of the same gang in New York.

'It's Spike speaking.'

'Yuh?' came Con's cautious voice.

'Say, Con, I want to see you. Shaun O'Donnell got his tonight and it looks as though this outfit is breaking up. Say, what's the chance of comin' over?'

Con O'Hara was not clever, but he shared with the lower animals a certain instinct of danger.

'Sure, there's a chance. See me in the morning, Spike. I've got a touch of grippe, and I ain't been out all night.'

'What's the matter with tonight?' asked Spike.

'What's the matter with the morning?' asked Con.

A pause, and then:

'Maybe, I'll call in and see you and take a chance . . .'

'You don't know what chance you'll take if you call on me tonight, kid,' said Con, and there was a significance in his tone not to be overlooked.

Spike Mulligan did a bit of quick thinking. Was O'Hara in or was he just one of these floating guerillas loosely attached to the Perelli crowd, that Tony sometimes employed?

Spike knew the day and hour of Con O'Hara's arrival in Chicago. The balance of probability was that Con was still a free-lance killer, as yet unprotected by Perelli's organisation.

'This guy won't be hard to get,' he said, 'and there'll be no rap coming.'

He was a little terrified of Mrs. O'Donnell—all the crowd were. To go back to her and report a failure would be to invite trouble. He made to where he had left his 'torpedoes' and after a hasty consultation they moved towards the block where Con O'Hara had his residence.

To get into the apartment was a simple matter. There was a janitor, who was also the elevator man. The front door was open day and night.

As they came in sight of the building they saw something else: a closed sedan came slowly from the direction of the city and pulled up within fifty yards of the entrance. The headlights were dim and became dimmer, and nobody alighted.

Spike halted in the shadows and grinned. To walk into that building was to invite himself to an insignificant funeral, for the honours of the day would go to Shaun. They went back to the place where his car was parked and drove towards Jimmy's house. If there was a car waiting here, there was nothing left for him to do but to return to his employer.

They drove past the building; there was no sign of car or guard. A hundred yards away Spike alighted, walked slowly back and, crossing the road, reached the closed door of the apartment house. To open the door was easy enough: he had lodged at the place himself and after his interview with Mrs. O'Donnell he had gone home and got the key.

The passage was dark. He went softly up the stairs to the third floor and knocked gently at Jimmy's door. There was no reply. He knocked again, listening intently. If Jimmy had moved in his bed, he would have heard him, but there was no movement, no creak of mattress or sound of stealthy footstep. He turned the handle, and when he found that the door was not locked he knew that the room was empty. Jimmy had not completely carried out instructions.

Spike switched on the light and looked round. The bed had been slept on, but not in; he read all the signs with a skill born of practice. Perelli had got him away. And then a sudden, queer premonition of danger sent a chill down his spine If Perelli had got his killer away, it was because he knew somebody was going after him.

He turned off the lights and went softly down the stairs, his gun arm stiffly extended, sensitive to every sound. Spike's thumb was on the backdrawn hammer of his Colt, the trigger tightly pressed. He had but to release his thumb and whosoever stood within the range of his gun died.

Turning the knob of the front door, he opened it and stopped. Immediately opposite, at the foot of the steps down which he must pass, was the sedan he had seen near Con O'Hara's house. He stood, thunderstruck, for a fraction of a second and then something hard and painful thumped against his spine.

'Step lively, Spike,' whispered a voice behind him.

He was pushed out on to the top step, and simultaneously two men came out of the car, one walked up to him and took away the gun from his hand, slipping his thumb under Spike's to lower the trigger gently.

'What's the idea?'

His throat was dry, his voice husky. He glanced up and down: no sign of his own torpedoes; they would be waiting for him two blocks away unless they had seen the car drive up. Maybe they were too dumb to see that.

The man behind him closed the door softly.

'You're going a ride, Spike,' he said.

He was pushed into the car by the side of the driver. The vehicle moved on.

'Say, what's the idea?' said Spike again. 'I was taking a message from Shaun to Jimmy.'

There was a chuckle from the seat behind him.

'Now maybe you can take a message from Jimmy to Shaun!' mocked the voice.

The car gathered speed, and Spike could do no more than sit and wonder just where they were heading for. Each gang had its favourite spot.

All thought, imagination, hope, human volition went out deafeningly. The driver slowed the car and drew up at the sidewalk. The man who had fired put down his pistol and, leaning over, flung open the door, lifted the dead man by the shoulders and heaved him on to the road, the car swerving scientifically to avoid its wheels' contact with the sprawling figure, and then it circled and went back the way it had come.

The killer lit a cigarette.

'Might have got him outside to do it,' grumbled the driver. 'It'll take all night to clean up this coat of mine.'

'Forget it,' said the killer.

'Or burn it,' said the other. 'Say, what are furnaces for?'

6

Mike Feeney came back from Indianapolis more worried than vengeful. There was nothing foolish about this slow-thinking man and, although perturbed and not a little terrified by the savage outburst which greeted him when he met his sister, he saw the situation, as every good racketeer must see it, from the aspect of Big Business.

'Spike didn't come back,' she stormed.

'Sure he didn't come back.'

He was relieved to be given this opportunity for asserting the superiority of his tactics.

'It was mad you were to send the three men to get O'Hara and Jimmy! Wouldn't Perelli be expectin' it? Arrah! Stop, will ye?' he roared, as she raised her voice again. 'There's only one way to fix Tony and I know it. Them boys will get theirs. I've said it, so stop your yellin', will ye?'

He sat down sulkily to a huge breakfast, a tired, harassed, ill-tempered man, for beyond and behind the immediate cause of his fury was the fear of death which comes to all men living as precariously near to the edge as he. Trying to recall all his associations with the Perelli crowd, he considered what were his points of contact with them.

Angelo . . . ?

He was friendly with Angelo, who had sought a fusion of interests, a merger that would have given Feeney control of a certain definite area. Mike was staging a birthday party at Bellini's, and Angelo had half promised that this should be a day of truce and that Perelli himself would come and talk heart to heart with his rival. It was to be an important gathering, with a sprinkling of judges to give tone and emphasise the note of propriety usually absent from such gatherings. By his own peculiar code and method

74

of reasoning he dissociated himself from that enmity of Perelli's which had brought Shaun to his inevitable end.

He breakfasted alone. His position was a serious one. There was no one to take Shaun's place; there were many matters to consider, his line of action to decide upon. His own life was dependent upon the decisions he took. . . .

Tony Perelli did not breakfast as early that morning.

When the sun was high, he sat at the organ seat, his fingers wandering over the keys aimlessly, his mind occupied with music to the exclusion of all other matters. Minn Lee sat on the lower step of the dais, working with stitches of microscopic precision the Chinese dragon she had been embroidering ever since she came to Tony's apartment. It was an amazingly complicated dragon, and she fashioned it without the guidance of a pattern. A thing of delicate shades, already beautiful. . . . Tony was proud of it and would stop in the middle of dinner and send for her to exhibit it to the admiration of the guests.

He stopped playing, swung his legs leisurely over the organ seat.

'You like that?' he asked.

She nodded.

He had come to set great store by her judgment, or perhaps he demanded the approval of his audience, and there was no audience like Minn Lee.

'Gounod,' he said. 'What a pity the damn' fool wasn't born an Italian! But he was educated in Rome. You wouldn't think I knew that?'

She looked up at him with that faint, inscrutable smile of hers. It meant just a little more than was apparent.

'You know everything, Tony.'

He smiled complacently. Minn Lee was the only person in the world who could make him purr.

'Of music—yes,' he said. 'Perhaps if I'd stayed in the orchestra at Cosmolino's I'd have been a swell musician, but I was ambitious. I became a cook! I was always an artist.'

This was nearly true.

He had never really been a cook, but found a perverted satisfaction in claiming his origin as being something more lowly than it was. None suspected Antonio Perelli of an inferiority complex, yet such was the fact. No man was more conscious of his social defects than this lord of the underworld. Once he had killed an ex-schoolmaster, a member of the old Dominic gang, who had twitted him about his handwriting and questioned his literacy.

Angelo Verona came in, very tired, not in the best of moods. He had been out since early morning, checking in a supply of the real stuff that had come through in the night. He slipped off his gloves, pulled off his overcoat, dropped it on the settle, took a bundle of papers from his pocket, and laid them on the table with an inquiring look at Minn Lee.

'Do you want me, Angelo?'

'Si,' he replied.

Tony stooped and pulled the girl to her feet.

'Run away, little Chinese angel: you come back by and by.'

Near the door the girl turned. Had Tony forgotten his promise? she wondered.

'You said you would come and sit in my room . . .' she began.

'I said I would see you by and by.' His voice rose to a shout. 'Damn it! Can't you hear me?'

That was like Tony—the Tony she had half learned. She smiled again and, turning obediently, left them. When she had gone:

'Well?' asked Perelli.

Angelo reported briefly.

'That train's through from Canada. One box car was opened and half the booze was gone.'

Ordinarily the news that a portion of his shipment had been hijacked would have been sufficient to arouse in him a raging tempest of fury. Tony was a bootlegger. Never in his life had he utilised his forces to steal other men's goods. By his understanding he was a square dealer. Every case of the liquor he imported, every beaker of alky was bought with real money. Hijacking was the long suit of the Feeney gang. Nothing was sacred to them. They would steal a shipload of other people's liquor in a night, had even broken into bonded warehouses with the connivance of certain officials, and removed large quantities of the stuff

76

without paying a cent. If Angelo had expected an outburst he was agreeably surprised.

'Half the liquor's gone, eh?' said Tony. 'I know all about that. It was the police in Michigan. I told them to help themselves.'

Angelo smiled grimly and consulted his notebook.

'Well, they have! And I paid five hundred dollars to the railway clerk. Two thousand dollars to that prohibition officer: he'd 'a' stopped it going out of the yard else.'

Tony said it was worth it. He didn't want trouble—that was his slogan. He didn't want trouble with the police, with the Federal authorities, with Feeney, or with any other gang.

'We'll start trucking it tomorrow,' said Angelo. 'It's all the best stuff.'

Tony glanced casually at the list. He noted one or two familiar names, and uttered a warning as he turned to the organ again.

'Be careful, Angelo,' he said, 'that Judge Cohlsohn gets that good champagne. Last time he got apple juice and he raised hell! I don't want no trouble with them Supreme Court judges. An' watch out for Feeney's crowd.'

He nodded and repeated: 'Watch out!'

Angelo smiled. He was young and confident. To him the blow which had befallen Feeney's relative and henchman was one from which the Irishman would never recover. Feeney was finished—the nibbled core of a greatness that was never too great.

'Forget it,' he scoffed. 'Feeney will be like a cat on wheels now that Shaun's got his. Shaun was the brains of that outfit.'

Tony smiled. He had other views, and it was typical of him that he did not express them even to a man who was as near to being completely in his confidence as any.

'That's the worst thing that's ever been said about Mike Feeney,' he said.

He sat at the organ and played a few notes of *Rigoletto*. He played softly and with feeling. *Rigoletto* soothed him, gave him something of gaiety. To Angelo the man was an enigma, outside the range of his experience, beyond under-

77

standing. He brought the conversation to another matter which was concerning him.

'O'Hara's a loud speaker, ain't he?'

Tony turned his head lazily.

'He's Irish, and he's from New York—he can't help it,' he said.

Piqued by his indifference, Angelo said:

'He's got some swell woman.'

The music stopped suddenly and Tony swung round on the organ seat. Here was a matter very vital. Women carried the colour of romance; they were the flowers in life's garden.

'Eh?' His eyes were alight, and Angelo groaned.

He himself had little or no interest in women. He loathed their intrusion into business. He was systematically offensive to them, Minn Lee alone being the exception. To Minn Lee his attitude had been curiously gentle—curious to those who knew Angelo Verona. He had gone out of his way to make life more agreeable for her. And now . . .

'I was a bonehead to talk about women,' he said. 'That's your trouble, Tony. Why can't you keep your mind on business for a few years and then take a holiday? About this stuff for the judge . . .'

But Tony Perelli was not to be put off.

'She's really pretty—this O'Hara woman? It's funny you should notice her. I don't think I remember you ever speaking of women before. And if you say she's pretty . . .'

'Ain't they all?' asked Angelo wearily. 'What's prettiness anyway? It's only a face.'

'Nize?' asked Tony, his eager eyes still fixed on the other.

'It depends,' said Angelo cautiously.

'Blonde?' said the other, and Angelo folded up his notebook deliberately.

'What made me talk about her I don't know,' he said in despair. 'It's the first time since Minn Lee has been here . . .'

'Leave her out.' Tony's voice was sharp. 'Tell me about this girl. Is she smart—*soignée*?'

Angelo shook his head.

'What the hell that is I don't know,' he said. 'All I can tell you is that she's tough but she's classy. She's the kind that you see here three days a week.'

But Tony pressed for detail. He had an uncanny perception for the extraordinary, and he knew that Mrs. O'Hara was something out of the ordinary run. But he had one doubt.

'O'Hara—that pig—how could he get a fine girl?' he demanded. 'He's fat, he's noisy, he's ignorant.'

'If you start wondering what girls see in guys, your mind is going right off your business,' said Angelo, and looked at his watch. 'O'Hara will be here in a few minutes. I had him on the wire this morning. Spike tried to see him in his apartment last night. Say, I'm glad that torpedo's dumb. He's a fool, and a fool can't be trusted to do the wrong thing all the time—sometimes he's on the spot by accident.'

With a shrug of his shoulders, Tony turned back to his organ. He heard the door shut on Angelo and five minutes later the shrill tinkle of a bell. Kiki was putting his breakfast on the table: thin slices of brown toast, a grapefruit and black coffee. Tony was abstemious in his diet. He dreamt of returning to the sylph-like proportions of his early youth.

'See to the door, Kiki,' he said, and presently he heard a loud voice in the hall outside, and smiled.

O'Hara! It wasn't possible that he should possess anything in the world that Perelli desired.

Con came into the apartment, looking spruce, shaven, jocular. He was conscious of a piece of work well done. He saw Tony at the organ and was rather amused. He despised the artistic side of Perelli's nature; his love for the organ was almost tantamount to effeminacy in the eyes of this dull gangster.

He had never stood in awe of Tony, felt a definite superiority to him. He had a Celt's misplaced disparagement for the Latin races—a disparagement more frequently found in those nearest of kin to the Latins than in the more sober and more modest Nordic strains. Listening now uncomprehendingly to the aria, his bull voice pierced the music.

'That's funny,' he chuckled. 'Playin' the organ like somep'n' in church. You had a guy singin' here yesterday. Foreign, wasn't he? And devil a word did I understand of it!'

79

Tony surveyed him coldly. Con was tolerable when he kept to his own plane. As a critic of music he was ludicrous; as a critic of Tony he placed himself outside the pale.

'That man sang at La Scala in Milan,' he said, but his information was without significance to his hearer.

'Gee! Them talkies is everywhere, ain't they?' he said admiringly. 'That guy certainly made me laugh!'

'It amused you?'

If Con had been better acquainted with Tony he would have seen the red light. It was not in this mood that Con O'Hara should have made his call. Tony had a genuine grievance. He had read four newspapers that morning and each journal had told the same story.

'Yuh. But I'm the sort of guy who gets a laugh out of most anything,' said Con.

They both heard the mournful wail of a siren. Tony got up and, going to the balcony, looked down into the street.

It was a police car speeding along Michigan Boulevard.

'Yuh,' said Con. 'They're busy this morning. Them bums ain't got nothin' else to do except to whoop around! Pardon me.' He stretched out his hand to take a piece of toast from the rack.

Tony's steel knife blade missed him by the fraction of an inch. Con drew back his hand with an oath and stared at the man who had dared to swing a knife to his finger. His eyes narrowed, his ugly, full face grew taut.

'What's the big idea?' he asked slowly.

'I am not asking you to breakfast, my friend,' said Tony. 'If you are hungry, I will ring for Kiki to give you something to eat. Have you read the newspapers this morning?'

He indicated the pile that lay on the table where his breakfast stood.

Con O'Hara did not read newspapers. They were, he said righteously, too full of lies for his liking, but Tony was insistent, and thrust a *Tribune* into his hand.

'On the top of the page, please look.'

Con read aloud with some difficulty, for he was no great scholar.

' "Shaun O'Donnell, booze racketeer, dies at hands of gunmen. Dead gangster Mike Feeney's chief aide. Put on the spot, Detective-Commissioner Kelly thinks . . ." ' He laughed. 'Put on the spot! Say, that'll make Feeney mad!'

Tony nodded. He had not killed Shaun to irritate his brother-in-law; life was too serious a matter to bother about the unimportant reactions of human beings.

'Go on,' he said, 'if you can read.'

O'Hara scowled at him and, taking up the newspaper again, spelt out the news.

' "Last night at twelve, Patrolman Ryan, of the Maxwell Street Station, heard shots, and, running in the direction, found the body of Shaun O'Donnell. He had been shot . . ." Hell, wasn't I there?'

Tony smiled.

'Yes, I believe you were there. That is why it's so very interesting—for me!'

The thick lips of Con O'Hara curled.

'The kid gave him one or maybe two, it doesn't matter much, because I was out of the machine with my rod up before the first shot was fired. I don't waste no time, Tony. It was all over and we was headin' for Michigan Avenue before that bull was in sight.'

Again Tony Perelli smiled.

'That was fine! And he was dead?'

'Was he dead!' scoffed the other. 'Listen, when I pull a rod on a guy, his front name's "late"!'

Perelli leant back in his chair, chewed at a golden tooth-pick.

'And yet,' he said suavely, 'he was alive when he was found.'

There was a silence painful to Con O'Hara.

'How's that?' he asked incredulously.

'He was alive,' said Tony, 'and taken to the Brothers' Hospital, and Harrigan saw him there. Gwan—laff!'

O'Hara was taken aback. He had skimmed the news-papers without reading them carefully, or he would have anticipated this reproach that had come to him, and he might have been more ready with his excuses.

'It was that college kid,' he said, 'I told you I didn't want to take him along. Say, that boy fell apart the minute he pulled his rod. I've never missed my man.'

Tony's smile was most amiable.

'I see. 'E missed him, but *you* killed him, and that was

why he was alive at one o'clock in the Brothers' Hospital with Mr. Harrigan saying: "Come clean for your old mother's sake." '

It was shocking news to O'Hara; an accusation of inefficiency in his own expert art. Killing was bread-and-butter work for him. He lived in comparative affluence on the strength of his ability to draw in the flash of an eye and shoot surely as soon as the muzzle of his gun was out of his pocket.

Tony was looking at him oddly.

'You come to me from New York—a swell killer from the Five Pointers. "In New York we do this—in New York we do that." In Chicago, sweetheart, I send you out to do a leetle, simple thing, and what do you do?'

O'Hara had his alibi ready:

'That kid got me . . . got me rattled,' he began.

'Sure he got you rattled,' interrupted Perelli. 'Swell feller, eh? All brains!'

The man turned on him, ugly with rage, and Perelli, an excellent judge of character though he was, and one who knew just where to stop, could not forbear another gibe.

'Well, he's dead now,' growled the man.

'Sure.' Tony showed his teeth in a delighted smile. 'Everybody dies some time. But when I mark a man he is not to die of old age! That is all.'

'Now listen . . .'

'That is all.' Perelli arrested further excuses. 'I am not annoyed, but Mike Feeney will be calling. I've been expectin' him all morning.'

Even as he spoke the telephone on the table buzzed. O'Hara reached for the receiver, but Tony took it from his hand.

'Not you, Con! You would go to answer the call of one man and find yourself talking to another!'

It was Mike Feeney, incoherent with anger, so lurid, so violent, that his words blasted on the delicate diaphragm. He was talking in the presence of his sister, Perelli guessed.

'Mr. Perelli is not at home . . .' he began, and there came a burst of profanity that made Perelli's delighted smile widen. 'Don't use such language, Mister Michael Feeney! I may be all those things, and yet the lady at the Central

might not like to hear you saying them. I tell you . . . I don't
. . . Listen, you silly Irish! I don't know anything about
Shaun O'Donnell. In the *Tribune* it says you put him on
the spot. . . . Oh, my friend, you are like a German opera.
I tell you I do not know . . . I swear to you by the blessed
Mother of God'—he crossed himself—'I do not know.
O'Hara? Don't be silly!'

'Tell him from me . . .' began Con, but Tony shot one
glance in his direction, and continued offensively.

'That New York man is too big a fool; I wouldn't trust
him to kill a cat. He's one of these guys who shoots out of
his mouth. Listen, Mike! Oh, listen!' And then his voice
turned to a snarl. 'You and your bunch of micks have been
musclin' in on my territory—yes, you have! Shaun was
the guy who shot up one of my speakeasies the other night,
an' who hijacked a carload of liquor from the Erie yards
—yuh, I know! I don't want no trouble. I tell you what
you're doing—you're ruining one grand business! Yuh? I
meet you at the corner of Michigan and 25th? An' where
do I go from there? To the undertaker's parlour? Say,
you're not goin' to put me on the spot? Why don't you
come here?'

Con, listening, became agitated.

'Don't you trust that guy . . .' he began, but Tony silenced
him with a scowl.

'All right, all right. I'll meet you—opposite the *Tribune*
building. That's O.K. by me. There'll be a machine-gun
covering you. I'm saying it. Sure I want to talk. And we'll
come back here. You an' me, without rods. O.K. Eleven
o'clock.' He hung up the receiver and pressed a bell on the
table.

'Now listen, I'm tellin' you somep'n' . . .' began O'Hara
as Angelo came in hurriedly.

'I am meeting Feeney,' said Perelli curtly. 'Arrange that
I am covered.'

He spoke in Italian.

'Feeney?' Angelo's eyes opened wide.

'Don't look like an imbecile,' said Perelli impatiently.
'Fix it! I've got to meet this man. There's no trouble comin'
today. Tomorrow, yes, the day after, sure! But today, no.
I will meet him. It will be very interesting!'

O'Hara listened impatiently to the staccato rattle of their Italian tongues. His sense of importance was impaired. His vanity was a tender plant growing in strange soil. Once or twice he tried to break in, but failed to impress his presence upon either of the men. He was conscious in his dull way that he was in his place—where he had been put. Just a servant of no great importance, he, Con O'Hara, a lieutenant of the Five Pointers!

'Say, I'm in this, ain't I?' he wailed, but they did not notice him. 'You don't know when you've got a good guy. Hey, Tony, you're not treating me square.'

When he was annoyed his voice rose to a roar: it was a bellow now.

Angelo turned his languid attention upon him, favoured him with a sustained and insolent stare.

'Do you want to see your woman?' he asked. 'She's in the hall, waiting for you.'

O'Hara did not see the look in Tony's eyes, or he might not have grinned so complacently. He was very proud of Maria, anxious to show her off, with certain reservations.

'I'll be right along,' he said, as Angelo went out of the door.

'Your woman?' Tony's voice was very friendly, soft, almost caressing. 'You have a woman, eh?'

O'Hara smirked.

'Sure. Ain't I a human being?'

Tony was looking at him thoughtfully.

'Nize, huh?'

O'Hara lifted his eyebrows in simulated surprise.

'Ain't you never met her, Tony?'

Nobody knew better than he that they had not met. To say that O'Hara dreaded such a meeting would be untrue; that he had felt a little uneasy at possible complications was nearer the mark. He knew Perelli by repute: he had a reputation and a past that was thickly studded with affairs in various hues of drabness. O'Hara, as a gangster, was a business man. He held to the traditions of the leaders who had made him—that women belonged to out-of-business hours.

'No, I have not seen her,' said Tony gently. 'She is pretty, eh?'

O'Hara nodded and grinned.

'She's dandy,' he said.

It was the first sign of real enthusiasm Perelli had seen in his new henchman.

And then it occurred to O'Hara to ask a question that had been on the tip of his tongue for some time.

'Say, Tony, I can't understand you runnin' around with a Chink.'

The smile left Perelli's face. The flush that had been excited by this new interest faded to his natural colour, which was something between brown and grey.

'I don't speak that language—Chink!'

He had ceased to be a friend. He was the master again. O'Hara felt the menace in his tone and wilted.

'Listen,' he said hastily. 'I'm not sayin' anything against Minn Lee. She's a swell-lookin' kid.'

The smile returned to Perelli's face. It was a surer way to gain his goodwill by praising his possessions than by flattering his own qualities.

'Sure,' he nodded. 'But not so nize as yours, eh?'

O'Hara did not say as much, but he thought so. A Chinese was a Chinese to him, something so definitely foreign that he could not place himself in the same category.

'Bring her in,' suggested Tony.

O'Hara hesitated.

'Would you like to meet her?' he asked, and when Tony signified that desire the old hesitancy came back.

Why did Perelli want to see her? He was wholly absorbed in Minn Lee and never betrayed the least wish to meet any new woman. O'Hara had seen him at parties with the loveliest girls present, entirely oblivious of their charms and their attractions.

He gave a note of warning, which he thought would be sufficient.

'She's crazy about me,' he said.

'She must be,' said Tony, but the sarcasm was wasted on the other. 'Go on, bring her in.' He half turned. 'I'll go,' he said, but O'Hara caught him by the arm.

'Here, wait a minute! I'll bring her. On the level, Tony.' His challenging eyes met his chief's.

'Sure, on the level.'

Perelli was amused. He read into this uneasiness a tribute to his own power of attraction, and was flattered. Probably a very dull woman, he thought, and yet that uncanny instinct of his . . .

'We are very fond of one another,' said Con slowly, 'and there's going to be trouble for anybody who tries to muscle in.'

'That is bad news.'

His remark was too subtle for the other to distinguish.

'Who's going to muscle in?'

'Well, I know what you Wops are,' growled O'Hara, and Tony showed his teeth.

'Wops—that is a nize word. Perhaps you can think of something better if I give you plenty of time.' He brought his hand down on the other's shoulder. 'Swell fellow, Con. I make plenty of money for you.'

As Con O'Hara went out, and the door closed softly behind him, Perelli's smile became a mask of concentrated malignity. He spat out a few words in Italian that were not so much uncomplimentary to Con O'Hara as to his relatives.

From his pocket he took a tiny gold bottle, pressed a spring and a fine powder of scented spray bedewed the lapels of his fashionable coat.

In a way Perelli was a fop. He loved beautiful things, fine scents. He imported the rarest perfumes for his own use. He washed his hands in rosewater and Angelo, a born economist, once calculated that Perelli's daily bath cost him twenty dollars.

He was facing the door when Con came back, but his eyes were for the woman who followed him into the room. Perelli was a man who dreamed about women, and never once had he met a type that was comparable with the supreme creature of his imagination. And now he had met her. Blonde, perfectly featured. He guessed her to be a Pole and was right. She was of the height, she had the figure, the bearing, of his lady of dreams, and from that moment there was no other creature in the world for him but this woman who called herself O'Hara but was in fact Maria Pouluski.

He stared at her as though she were a materialised spirit

and in a dream he heard O'Hara's harsh voice:

'Meet Mr. Perelli, Maria.'

The hand that rested in his was small and soft, the fingers long and tapering. He held it for a moment and then, bending, kissed it. If her voice was harder than he hoped to hear, it did not shatter the illusion. There was music in it of a kind, a certain sugary sweetness which belonged to the polite conventions.

'I've heard a whole lot about you, Mr. Perelli,' she said.

Con was looking at them both. His big, round forehead was screwed up in a frown.

'Sure, I'm always talkin' about you—ain't I, kid?'

He had talked a lot about Perelli, but not all of it was complimentary; some of it was distinctly unflattering. He had spoken of Tony as an equal. Now she was to see him graded.

The girl was uncomfortable at his silence, but greatly flattered by all she read in his eyes. Maria Pouluski was a quick thinker. She saw opportunities and possibilities that had been beyond all her dreams. Con had talked about him, yes, but she could remember only one thing: 'That guy must be worth ten million dollars, twenty maybe.' And here was the man, staring at her, like one of those admirers who used to call at the stage door and want to take her to supper.

'I'd like to know Mrs. Perelli,' she said. 'She's a Chinese lady, isn't she?'

Tony turned his head slowly in the direction of his gunman, and smiled grimly.

'Chinese lady, you hear that, Irish? She didn't say "Chink". She said "Chinese lady". Will you remember that, please?' He turned to the girl. 'Yes, she's fifty-fifty, Chinese-American.'

He put out his arms and for a moment she thought he was going to embrace her, and her heart missed a beat. She had no illusions about Con. He was slow in all movements except with his gun. He could draw and shoot so quickly that none could follow the movement of his hand.

But Perelli was loosening the coat from her shoulders.

'Let me take this,' he said, held it up for a moment and looked at it with smiling contempt.

87

O'Hara was getting restless, watching him with growing anger.

'We'll step out now, if you're ready, Maria,' he said loudly, but Tony ignored him.

'You like Chicago?'

She nodded.

'It certainly is a swell place.'

'Better than New York?' he asked, and again looked at the coat on the settle. 'We have beautiful stores, good furs, sables on chiffon. Exquisite. We will do some shopping one day.'

O'Hara stood, undecided: how far could hospitality justify this blatant invitation? He did not know Tony well enough to resent this friendliness. Wops were notoriously polite, given to empty promises that meant nothing.

'Perhaps,' Tony went on, 'we shall see some sables.'

Her gurgling laugh was music to his ears.

'Sables! Say, what are you handing me?'

She, too, was conscious of Con's disapproval and she turned to him for support.

'Your friend, Mr. Perelli, is a swell kidder. Why, I've only had that model . . .' She looked at the coat.

Until that morning she had been rather proud of it. Now it was inexplicably shabby. She saw where it was worn on the sleeve. The model was only a year old.

Con O'Hara felt it was the moment to justify himself.

'That coat set me back two thousand dollars,' he said deliberately.

Tony laughed.

'Two grand! I pay that for the fur collars!'

Angelo came in and Tony caught his eye; the Irishman was too busy and too ostentatiously looking at his watch to notice the signal.

'Gee, look at the time!' He was a bad actor. 'Come on, kid. We shan't make that appointment.'

'You're wanted on the wire, Con.'

Angelo was unusually polite. Not often did he address O'Hara by his Christian name.

'Me?' incredulously. 'Who is it? Nobody knows I'm here. . . . Can't you put it through here?'

Angelo looked at him and made a mysterious signal.

'Police Department,' he said under his breath. 'That's what it sounded like. Maybe they know you're here.'

'Kelly knows everything,' said Tony.

O'Hara hesitated. The one thing he did not want to do was to leave his wife alone in the salon with Perelli. He looked from her to Tony, helpless with doubt.

'Don't keep that man waiting,' said Perelli. 'You stay here, Mrs. O'Hara—you shall see Chicago from my balcony.'

He looked at Con through half-closed eyelids.

'Why are you waiting?' he asked sharply.

The girl understood: spurs for Con. She, at any rate, had no illusions. This matter was progressing in such a direction as she could wish. She was curious to discover what method of approach there would be. She hardly noticed that her husband had left the room.

There was much to admire in this great salon: the paintings were exact copies from the Doge's Palace, the white marble arch of the balcony and the slim Venetian pillar that supported it.

'It's a swell dump, Mr. Perelli; almost like a church. I ain't seen one like it since I left . . .' She did not particularise the city, the state or the continent where she had seen a cathedral interior.

She stepped out on the balcony and suddenly an arm was put round her. Tony's hand was under her chin and her head was forced back, and their lips met. She was unprepared for this. A swift worker. She struggled a little; he did not hold her long enough to give her indignation scope, but she breathed with difficulty when he released her.

'You've got a nerve! You've never seen me before!' she said breathlessly.

'You like this place?' he asked eagerly. 'Swell, eh? Where do you live, Maria?'

The man was aflame. His eyes burned her. The pressure of his hands on her shoulders hurt.

'Where do you live?'

Struggling from his grasp, she walked backward from him.

'We've got an apartment off State,' she said.

'Four rooms and a bath!'

'Well, it's good enough for me!'

'Nothing's good enough for you!'

He caught her again. Her lips were too conveniently placed for any reluctant woman.

'You've got a nerve to kiss me like that!' she whimpered. 'If Con saw you do this . . .'

'Con!' he exploded.

He swung her round fiercely, still gripping her shoulder, lowered his face to hers, searching her eyes.

'If Con knew! I will do it before him and want nothing better!'

He was trembling, his voice was slurred. Never in her life had Maria Pouluski made so instant, so terrific an impression. She was thrilled, a little terrified.

'Are you crazy?' she gasped. 'He'd kill you . . .'

He laughed. Somebody said that Tony Perelli had too keen a sense of humour to be dangerous. To know him well was to discover that he was never quite so deadly as when he was amused.

'If he killed me I would be crazy,' he said, and suddenly released her and snatched from his little finger a ring with a glittering bluish-white stone. 'Look. Take this!'

She gaped at the jewel, tried to draw back, but he seized her hand and forced it on her finger.

'Take it!'

Did he mean it? She was in a panic lest he was fooling her.

'I couldn't. . . . Oh, it's lovely!'

Five thousand dollars, much more. On her finger it seemed the size of a nut, a big, white, glittering, beautiful thing that flashed all the colours of the spectrum.

'It's yours,' said Tony, 'Perhaps I will give you another one like it.'

She gazed down at the ring, awe-stricken.

'Oh, momma!' she breathed. 'Isn't it swell!'

'Tonight I give a party,' he spoke rapidly: Con might be back at any moment. 'All the best people will be here, huh? You shall come—and Con.'

'Well, Con says . . .' she began.

'Con! Con!' impatiently. 'You'll come.'

'If Con . . .' she began again.

'Yeah, he'll come.' Tony nodded and looked at the door. 'You'll sleep here—there are plenty of rooms: seven, eight nobody uses. I will give you a suite near my study.'

She made one last desperate effort to regain a similitude of respectability.

'You ain't going to talk to me like that, Tony Perelli,' she said. 'Staying here . . . !' She had sunk down into the luxurious couch. 'Say, don't think because you've got all the money in the world . . . You've got a damn' nerve!'

'Sables on chiffon,' said Tony urgently. 'I pay fifty dollars for a pair of stockings—a hundred. Do you want money?'

Impetuously he drew a handful of bills from his pocket. For a moment she was frightened.

'God Almighty! What do you think I am?'

She was in his arms again, his mouth devouring hers; and then a sound in the hall outside brought him to his feet.

Con came in, glowering suspiciously. For a moment he stood at the door, surveying them.

'What's the idea?' he asked slowly. 'Headquarters didn't want me at all.' His dull gaze was fixed on Maria. 'What's the matter with you?' he growled.

There was reason for the question. Her face was flushed, her eyes unusually bright. He came back to an atmosphere of mystery, but a mystery that even he could solve.

She forced a laugh, and thrust out her hand.

'Look what Mr. Perelli gave me.'

He looked at it and then slowly raised his eyes to Perelli's.

'Oh, he gave you that, did he? Why?'

Tony Perelli supplied the answer.

'I give her two more if I wish. She is your wife, that's why.' He slapped O'Hara on the back—he was a better actor than the Irishman. 'This is a swell feller, Maria. I'll call you that. You must call me Tony, eh? He shall be in my place. I can trust him—nobody else. He is a Big Shot, sure!'

O'Hara was mollified. He was a very simple man. The prospect of immediate gain meant more to him than most things. He could fortify himself by his faith in the woman he called his wife, and yet . . .

'That's all right by me.' He surveyed Maria critically, a little menacingly.

A telephone bell rang and Tony Perelli went across to the table to answer it.

Slowly O'Hara came to the woman.

'Did that Wop get fresh with you?' he asked in a low voice. 'Try to kiss you or anything?'

'Why, no, Con! I'd like to see him start!'

Her surprise and indignation would not have deceived most men. Con was half convinced.

'That guy goes plum crazy over a skirt,' he said, 'if it's the right kind. Not everybody's his kind. You ain't! Say, he's mad about Minn Lee ...'

'That's good news,' said a soft voice, and he looked round.

Minn Lee had come quietly into the room and was standing at his elbow.

Agreeable drama for Maria. She looked at the slim little figure appraisingly. Some of these Chinese women could be pretty—there was a girl who went to the public school in Brooklyn and another girl she had seen in one of these Chinese restaurants in New York—but here was one not entirely Chinese. It puzzled her. She was a little too dumb to analyse the subtle difference between Minn Lee and all the Chinese women she had met. But there it was, to be felt if not understood. Something so obvious that it defied analysis.

Tragedy for Minn Lee. She had been watching Tony at the telephone, his eyes fixed on the girl. She knew that look; more important, she knew his type. That was a curious circumstance, for Tony had only vague notions of what pleased him, could never define exactly his fleshly requirements.

O'Hara beamed at the girl: here was relief from a strain which was becoming intolerable.

'Maria, met Mrs. Perelli,' he said.

Maria took the little hand in hers and, in the manner of her kind, was fulsome and unreserved in her flattery. Minn Lee's dress was beautiful—she said so. Minn Lee was unusually lovely that morning—she said as much.

Minn Lee, eyeing her gravely, realised that the inevitable woman had arrived. She could be philosophical in all matters but this. Perhaps there was in her heart some des-

92

perate hope that she might turn the trick by her own values. Had she been judging another woman's struggle to retain her man, she would have offered an exact prognosis of the course this love disease would follow.

Tony watched and swelled with gratification: two marvellous women—they were fighting for him. Not visibly, not so that a dull clod of a man like O'Hara could see or hear the clash, but clearly and unmistakably in Perelli's eyes, and when Maria drawled, 'I do admire your wife, Mr. Perelli,' he knew the battle had opened.

'Pretty, eh?' he smiled and laid his hand caressingly on Minn Lee's shoulder. 'Madame Butterfly, huh?'

Maria looked at him blankly.

'Is that so? Why, then I've heard about Mrs. Perelli . . .'

O'Hara came clumsily to her rescue:

'Don't be dumb, kid. Madame Butterfly is a dame in a book.'

'Madame Butterfly was Japanese.' Minn Lee came to the rescue of both, explained the mythical madame's place in literature. . . . 'Puccini—Tony will play.'

'Maybe tonight,' Tony jumped in quickly.

He was watching Maria.

'What do you think of her? Cute, eh? Show Maria your rings, honey.'

Obediently the girl put out her hand, and Perelli took it, indicating with his stubby forefinger all the evidences of his generosity. Rings, bracelets—he catalogued them, giving their price with assumed carelessness.

Maria listened dumbfounded, staggered by the figures he quoted. Minn Lee said nothing. She heard her possessions appraised, her sable wraps, her new ermine coat. Tony was frank even on the subject of more intimate wear, for which he paid fabulous figures. And she had all the money in the world.

Maria looked from the Chinese girl to Tony, from Tony to the stocky Irishman, from the Irishman to this gorgeous apartment and all that it stood for: social advancement, power, money. And she made her decision.

She had never made a decision that required less consideration, had fewer 'ifs' or 'buts' to it, and O'Hara's price as a gun fighter and leader she had already discounted.

Shrewdly she lined him up and placed him just where he belonged. He was a big wheel in the machine, but here was the driving power. She looked at the ring on her hand furtively. White stone; four carats or a little more; fifteen hundred dollars a carat—six thousand dollars. She had staked her claim.

Hardly she listened to what Tony was saying: Minn Lee had two sable wraps and all the money in the world. That was the way Tony Perelli treated his women; he was just like that—a woman could take anything she wanted from him. All the time she was conscious that his sly eyes were glancing sideways at her.

O'Hara heard and in a confused way understood. Men had been complimentary to Maria before, and he had been flattered. His reputation was such that they had never stepped over the line. Besides, it was the unwritten law that skirt was never to interfere with business. Women were chattels in his world. He had had his interest in the 'houses', had split profits from them. One could have isolated affections, as a man with a stable of horses might have his pet amongst them and feel a genuine regret when circumstances made him sell or slaughter it. It was the unusualness of this complication which disturbed him more than any active feeling of jealousy.

'We'll be steppin' out,' he growled.

Tony suddenly became aware of his presence.

'I want you, Con,' he said. 'Go, get that Jimmy boy. Your wife can stay till you come back. Minn Lee, you show Mrs. O'Hara the Winter Garden—that's where we have our parties,' he explained to her.

'Some other time, I guess,' grumbled the Irishman. 'Mrs. O'Hara's got an appointment. Snap into it now!'

For a moment Tony seemed likely to assert his authority.

'Oh, well. Au revoir.' He took Maria's hand. 'You will come to the party?'

She caught Con's eye and it said 'no'.

'I'm not so sure that I can . . .' she began.

'You come and you stay here. Minn Lee, we shall give Maria that suite on the Avenue.'

It was a command. Again she sought encouragement from Con and did not find any.

94

'We only live eight blocks away,' she hesitated.

Tony smiled.

'You will stay with us.'

'I don't like sleepin' in strange apartments,' interrupted O'Hara.

Perelli surveyed him coldly.

'Sing Sing was like 'ome to you?' he sneered.

There was trouble coming. Maria sensed it. The Chinese girl stood in the archway that led to the balcony. She knew it too. Trouble—tragic trouble. No new experience for her.

She smiled mechanically as the woman approached her, half turned with a little gesture to display the view.

To Con O'Hara here was an opportunity to assert his point of view. Tony was pulling at his cigar, watching the women thoughtfully, apparently oblivious of the man's presence until he stepped up to him.

'I'd like a word with you.' He lowered his voice so that it would not carry to the balcony. There was a menace in the tone.

An ordinary man might have quailed before it, but Tony Perelli was not an ordinary man. He knew exactly what this husband had to say, but there were certain things about him which were irritating: the faint odour of stale whisky and cheap perfume, for example. Slowly he brought his eyes from the balcony to the man who confronted him.

'Don't come so close, my frien',' he said softly.

'Get this straight.' O'Hara's blunt forefinger waved warningly in his face. 'There's going to be no . . .'

'You're crowding me.' Tony's voice was almost a caress.

He did not budge, but O'Hara edged closer. His face was within a few inches of Tony's.

'You leave Maria alone . . .'

Perelli took the cigar from his mouth and, with such deliberation that the man could not realise what he was doing, pressed the lighted end against O'Hara's face. The Irishman leapt back with an oath. It burned horribly. His hand went up to his cheek to brush away the ashes.

'Don't crowd me,' said Perelli.

For a moment O'Hara was paralysed with rage, but even in his fury he saw that Perelli's disengaged hand was in his

95

pocket, and there came to him for the first time in his life a sickening sense of fear.

'You're a hell of a guy in Chicago,' he said breathlessly, 'but Con O'Hara has told a whole lot of Big Shots where they get off!'

Tony shook his head. He was smiling.

'I never tell anybody where they get off,' he said smoothly. 'I put them off. If I want your woman I'll take her. You understand? I don't want no trouble. Widows are safer than wives, even wives who are not married. Don't be a fool.' He patted the other on the shoulder. 'You're a swell feller—a nize feller. I look after you.'

O'Hara was commanded; he fell back into the ranks of the subservient. He was hurt, but he could show this guy that a little thing like that didn't mean a lot to a right feller. And it was easier to accept the situation as it was interpreted for him than to analyse the causes. He forced a laugh.

'That's all right by me,' he said, and turned, beckoning Maria. 'Good-bye, Mrs. Perelli. Glad to have you know my wife.'

He had the illusion of having bridged an embarrassing moment with a certain amount of dignity.

He pushed Maria into his car and sat down in the driver's seat beside her. Not until he reached his house, and his blue-chinned chauffeur had relieved him of the car, did he become aware of her presence, and not until they were in their apartment, behind a locked door, did he speak.

'There will be no party tonight,' he said.

'Is that so?' she answered politely.

'That—is—so.' He was emphatic.

She shrugged her pretty shoulders.

'That's O.K. by me, Con, but you'll have to tell Mr. Perelli . . .'

'Don't worry what I'll tell Perelli,' he snarled. 'You ain't going to any party tonight.'

He called Tony on the phone.

'Say, Tony, you'll have to excuse Mrs. O'Hara tonight—she's sick.'

'I'll have a doctor here,' said Tony's cold voice. 'Bring her. And I asked you to get Jimmy. Where is he?'

'Listen . . .' began O'Hara, but the click of the receiver at Tony's end terminated the conversation.

He had his own affairs to occupy the day. Reprisal was not coming immediately from the Feeney gang. Preparations were going forward to give Shaun O'Donnell his grand exit to Mount Carmel, and while the preliminaries of this holy event were being fixed, it was the unwritten law that there should be a truce.

He went to the address where he knew Jimmy was staying and found that, contrary to all instructions, McGrath had gone out. He found him walking disconsolately along Michigan Boulevard, without escort, seemingly uncaring for the risk he ran; although, as Con knew, the danger was not very great.

He saw the boy walking ahead of him and, stepping up behind, slapped him on the back. Jimmy jumped round, white to the lips, his face twitching.

'Say, what's the matter with you?' scoffed Con, consciously superior to such an ignoble emotion.

'Nothing, only . . .'

'Tony wants you. What's the matter with you, Jimmy?' Jimmy shook his head.

'I don't know. Tired, I guess. I didn't sleep very well.' Con was amused.

As they strolled towards Perelli's apartment he revealed his own reactions to such adventures. They might have been reduced to the philosophy of Lady Macbeth.

'These affairs must not be thought about this way—so it would drive you mad.'

Jimmy listened, unhearing. He saw only the pained, puzzled look in Shaun O'Donnell's eyes that he had seen all the night, would see to the end of his days—the mute reproach of a murdered friend.

7

Minn Lee said very little after their visitors had gone. She sat stitching at the embroidery frame, her mind apparently intent upon her work. Tony lay on the couch, the stub of a cigar in one corner of his mouth, a newspaper in his hand.

'She is lovely,' said Minn Lee suddenly, apropos nothing. 'Very lovely.'

He put down the paper, looked at her and sat up, swinging his legs to the ground. There was no need for him to ask her of whom she was speaking.

'Yeah, she's swell,' he agreed.

Another long pause and then:

'You going to the opera tonight, Tony?'

He shook his head.

'Tonight is *Das Gotterdammerung*. I would rather go to the Zoo than hear Wagner!'

Her eyes were fixed on his.

'Maybe you will stay with me some time tonight?' she asked. 'I never see you. And I don't know where you go.'

He got up, coming towards her, and surveyed her thoughtfully.

'Leetle darling,' he said softly, 'how often have I said: "Think if you must think, speak if you must speak, but never let your thoughts and your tongue come together." Silly little devil!'

He pinched her cheek and she flinched.

'That hurts?' he asked, and she nodded. He pinched harder.

'And that?'

'You know,' she said, and her very meekness infuriated him.

'Why don't you cry when I hurt you, you heathen?'

98

He sat down in a chair near her, so near that by a slight movement she was sitting at his knees.

'Do you know what I am afraid of?' she asked.

'What every woman is afraid of—another woman,' he said.

In an hour his whole attitude towards her had undergone a revolutionary change. All the time she had known him he had not given even an indication that he was not completely devoted to her. If she had been wholly Western this amazing *volte face* would have terrified her, but she was Eastern, understood men well enough to accept ugly miracles.

'There *is* another woman?'

His gesture was half serious, half humorous.

'To me all women is another woman,' he said lightly.

Another pause.

'You used to stay with me nights—once.'

He sighed impatiently.

'I was fond of Quaker Oats—once. Now I eat puffed rice. Some day I go back to Quaker Oats.'

He meant that this answer should definitely end all discussion, but she was not to be silenced.

'I get a little scared sometimes,' she said with a little catch in her voice. 'About you, Tony. When you go out I never know if you will come back.'

' 'Itherto I 'ave.' he said curtly.

'That night they shot at you—I thought I'd die . . .'

'What is more important, I thought *I* would,' he said, 'but I didn't. An' where is Camona, an' Scalesi, an' clever McSweeney who shot me—all in 'ell! That is theologically accurate.'

And now she put into words for the first time the plan she had formed.

'Can't we get away from Chicago?'

He looked at her oddly.

'Sure—you can go by the Twentieth Century. You have time to make the reservations.'

'I said "we",' she began.

He got up and pulled her urgently to her feet.

'We is not me. You are just you, understand? Nothing but. You are like the furniture. I like you—you are pretty, charming and lovely to my eyes, but so are all the things in the apartment. Yet they do not say "we", huh? They do not say: "Tony Perelli, take us to Europe wit' you," huh?'

He took her face in his hand and kissed her on the mouth. He kissed her again and then struck her gently on the cheek.

'Damn' fool!'

She smiled, became herself again, but her brightness was forced and he knew it.

'Who is coming tonight?'

'You shall see them when they arrive. It will be a lovely party.'

'Will there be women?' she asked.

'I said it would be a lovely party'—curtly.

'She is coming?'

There was a vehement protest in her voice.

He nodded. There could only be one 'she'—Maria Pouluski. Yes, she was coming. Sick, eh? O'Hara had better be careful.

'Sure.'

'Why can't she stay away? She has her own man.' The voice of Minn Lee trembled.

'Did you see her own man?' he sneered.

'Yes, I saw him.'

'Well, wouldn't you go to a party if he was your man?' he demanded.

'Jimmy says . . .'

He turned his head at this.

'Oh, Jimmy! You like that college boy? He's nize?'

She nodded.

'Yes, he's nice. He's like a little baby to me.'

Something in her tone arrested his attention.

'Yuh! You take him in your arms like a little baby!' He caught her up to him savagely. 'And you kiss him, eh?'

He was a little breathless. Even in the exhilaration of his unfaithfulness he could feel the sharp pain of jealousy. Because of it perhaps. The pasha in him was not ready to let her go to another man. She was still his property, not to be surrendered.

So he held her with savage force against him and she could recover the illusion of her power over him.

'Like a little baby! Huh! Such things I have 'eard!'

100

He thrust her away, holding her at arms' length, searching her face suspiciously.

Jimmy?

He could not feel sore with Jimmy. And yet there was something he could not fathom.

'Why do you look at me like that?' he asked.

He heard the tinkle of the bell and released her slowly.

It was Con O'Hara, and with him the boy who at that moment occupied his thoughts. He gave Jimmy one swift, comprehensive glance. The boy was pale, peaked, nervous. Here was somebody to be gentled. He had taken it worse than he had anticipated. Tony had had his report the night before. Naturally Jimmy had fallen apart. It was his first killing. But he was staying apart—that was a little disconcerting.

'Hullo, Jimmy boy!'

Jimmy gave him a nod.

'I met him on the Avenue,' said O'Hara, and glanced significantly at Tony.

If that look was intended to warn Perelli that his new recruit was a failure, the warning came too late.

'I wanted to talk to you, Tony,' said Jimmy in a low voice.

To Minn Lee he offered a wintry smile that came and faded instantly.

'Run away, sweetheart.' Tony put his arm round her, guided and pushed her towards the door. 'Me and Jimmy has got something to say to one another.'

She turned, faced Jimmy. She had also something to say.

'Can I see you before you go?'

'Sure,' answered Jimmy.

Could she see him before he went? Why? What had she to tell him? Here was a matter for cogitation.

'Sit down,' he said.

Jimmy was wandering restlessly to and fro.

'I guess I'll walk around,' he said.

Tony smiled.

'That carpet set me back ten grand, but what's the use if you don't walk on it? Go to it, Jimmy.'

'He wants to have a little talk,' said O'Hara confidentially.

Tony nodded.

'Sure. My ears are very good. I heard him say so quite well.'

But O'Hara was snub-proof.

Jimmy found it difficult to start.

'I made a damned fool of myself last night . . .' he began.

Tony slipped his arm in the boy's and paced towards the balcony.

'That was nothing, boy. You're a swell feller. Don't worry. Who ain't made fools of themselves in this outfit?'

He waited. Jimmy had drawn himself clear and was walking up and down alone, his hands thrust into his pockets, his chin on his chest.

Presently . . . hesitantly . . .

'You see, I knew Shaun—rather liked him—and when I pulled on him . . . he looked at me . . . kind of hurt . . . you know like killing a dog you're fond of . . .'

Tony soothed him.

'I know just what you feel, kid, but it's nothing.'

'If Con hadn't been there,' the boy went on, 'I guess I'd have got myself bumped off rather than do it.'

Con beamed at this testimonial to his solid support.

'But I fixed him good, chief'—he was eager to impress— 'I'm not the kind of guy to let you down. I see the kid was nervous . . .'

Tony snapped round at him.

'Yuh? I listen to you, Con, plenty—in a minute. Yes, Jimmy?'

'I haven't slept. . . . I've been seeing him all night. . . . His eyes . . . looking like . . .' He stared at something he saw but was seen by no other in the room.

O'Hara felt it was the moment to offer a comment.

'Aw, can it! You ain't yeller, are ye?'

This time he could not mistake Tony's mood. The Sicilian's face was white with anger.

'You're dumb—be it!' He patted Jimmy on the back very gently, very encouragingly. It was the gesture of the elder brother. 'You're O.K. with me, Jimmy. Sure, I know how you feel. You're a college boy, huh? All that raw stuff don't look good. But we gotta do it, Jimmy. I don't want no trouble—I'd work this booze racket without hurting a fly if they'd let up on me. There's no sense to it, Jimmy, killin' and killin' and killin'. Who the hell wants to kill anybody? But they won't leave you be. You get all set and workin' fine an' dandy, smooth an' friendly an' everything, and then one of the North Side guys comes musclin' in, and you've *gotta* tell him where he gets off.'

'Say, that's the straight of it,' broke in Con. 'If you hadn't bumped him, he'd 'a' bumped you. I wised you up to that before we stepped out on it.'

Perelli's patience was deadly.

'Con, I don't like guys who talk such a hell of a lot, especially when I'm talking. Have you seen Kelly yet?'

'Don't worry about the cops,' said the irrepressible Irishman, 'they don't mean a damn' thing. Let me talk to Kelly.'

Jimmy heard the siren and saw Tony step on to the balcony and look down.

When he came back:

'Let you talk to him—he'll let you: that's his car. Ever meet this man?'

'Kelly? Ah-ha.' Con was smiling. 'No. Listen, chief, they're all alike ...'

'Don't call me chief, damn you!' He turned to Jimmy. 'Listen, Jimmy. You've got brains. Get this and get it quick: don't let this guy ball you up. Just say as little as you can.'

Jimmy was aghast.

'He's not going to ask me questions? He doesn't know it was me?'

'He won't unless you tell him. Don't stand for his bluff.'

'I'll talk to him,' Con nodded.

Perelli's eyes narrowed.

'You will, eh? Con, you're a grand spieler; I like you. You're swell, but don't talk, and don't get fresh. This ain't New York—this is America!'

Assistant Commissioner Kelly came slowly into the room. To Jimmy he was Fate and Nemesis. A tall, broad-shouldered man, with hard inscrutable eyes that shone behind horn-rimmed glasses, he brought with him an atmosphere which was strange and honest and menacing.

He was The Law, derided, held in contempt, non-existent if you believed in the Tonys and the Shaun O'Donnells of life. Yet it existed, and this man brought it with him, a dim and terrible reality.

The Detective Commissioner looked round from one to the other. His gaze was leisurely; there was a certain reluctant amusement in his eyes as though he saw a funny side of the situation.

''Morning, Chief,' Tony saluted him with a beaming smile.

'Having a party?' Kelly asked the question innocently. He was looking at Jimmy now.

'A little early for a party,' said Perelli brightly, and the chief nodded.

'I went to a party this morning'—his voice was dry, almost harsh; no longer was he amused. 'There was me and the coroner and Shaun O'Donnell. Me and the coroner did all the talking.'

To Tony's face came an expression of the deepest sadness.

'Poor old Shaun! Ain't that too bad! When I read the papers and saw he'd gone, why, I was just beaten. It spoilt my morning.'

Again that curt nod of Kelly's.

'It spoilt his,' he said drily. 'Is this boy McGrath?'

Tony introduced them, though the introduction was unnecessary.

'Mr. James McGrath—of Harvard. A college man,' he added.

Kelly knew well enough what was the social standing of Jimmy McGrath.

'Expelled in his first year for theft from another freshman. Is that right?' He jerked the question to the boy, sullen, silent, wholly terrified.

'You seem to know it all,' he said, and hardly recognised his own voice.

'He's making a fresh start, Chief,' Tony volunteered the information, and Kelly's lips curled.

'Huh? If I ever laughed, I'd laugh! Fresh start! What's he doing—painting lilies on bottles? That's not what you're doing, is it, kid?'

Jimmy did not answer.

'It wasn't what you were doing last night, was it?'

Jimmy took in a quick breath.

'I don't know what you're aiming at,' he said huskily.

The detective was concentrating his attack on the boy. Perelli had expected nothing less. He might suspect Con O'Hara, but Con could wait.

That Irishman listened with growing impatience. He might be suspected, might glorify in the suspicion, but it hurt him to be ignored.

There was another reason for his impatience: Jimmy was on the verge of a collapse and on the least excuse he would fall apart. Con had no illusions. Why did not this granite-faced man tackle *him*? He had been lined up before, knew the ways of policemen, knew the bluff of them; if the truth be told, knew their limitations. It was years since he, as an unimportant gangster, the newest recruit to the bad men, had been beaten up in old New York station house where later a police captain, one Becker, was to answer inconvenient questions from a sceptical district attorney.

'How long have you been in this racket?' asked Kelly.

Jimmy shifted uneasily.

'Which racket?' he began.

'It's O.K., Jimmy,' Tony's silky voice broke in. 'The Chief knows we're runnin' booze. Chicago never voted dry. He's been with me three months, Mr. Kelly. A nize boy . . .'

'Did you know Shaun O'Donnell?' asked Kelly.

'Yes, I've seen him.'

'Did you know him?' persisted the detective.

Jimmy nodded.

'You used to go to Bellini's and lunch with him, didn't you? Knew him pretty well?'

Jimmy hesitated.

'Yes, I knew him.'

'The boys tell me he and you were good friends. You used to go around together, didn't you?'

Jimmy McGrath set his teeth: he did not want to be reminded of that.

'Yes, I knew him,' he repeated.

'Know he's dead?' asked Kelly.

Jimmy nodded.

'Know that he was shot down last night by a grand

105

American sportsman?' the merciless detective went on, his eyes never leaving the other's. 'Just shot down by one of those cheap yellow droppers?'

There was no answer from Jimmy.

'I don't know what brothel his mother came from'—he was watching the boy so closely that not even the flick of his eyelid escaped attention—'but she bred an up and up fellow. Like mother, like son, eh?'

Jimmy's face went from white to red and from red to white again.

'What in hell have mothers got to do with it?' he began, and then he caught Tony's eye and understood the warning.

'Mothers have a lot to do with it,' went on Kelly slowly. 'I'd like to bet she's been through my hands; I ran the vice section for a year.'

The veins were standing out on the boy's forehead, his hands were clenched and his knuckles were white.

'Only a son of that kind of woman . . .'

'By God! If you . . .'

He was out of hand now. Tony stepped in swiftly.

'Jimmy!' His voice was a roar. 'Why can't you take his little joke?'

Kelly's hands were thrust into his pockets. He turned and faced the Big Shot, his voice was like ice.

'Perelli, you're a big noise in this city. You've got juries in your pocket and judges eat out of your hands. But if you interfere with me, I'll make trouble for you.'

Tony shrugged his broad shoulders.

'Interfere, Chief? Why, I only . . .'

'I know, I know,' said Kelly. 'You've done what you wanted to do: you've given him time to take a hold of himself. O.K., kid. You just tell me something, and come clean.'

He was close to the boy now. His hand shot out and got him on the chest, pushed him down on the sofa.

'Where were you last night?'

'At the theatre,' said Jimmy.

'Which theatre?' asked the detective.

'Why . . .' he hesitated. 'At the Blackstone.'

'At the Blackstone.' Kelly nodded. 'What was the number of your seat?'

106

Here O'Hara came into the scene. The questions were getting particularly dangerous, more dangerous because of the panic in Jimmy McGrath's eyes.

'Say, how in hell can he remember?' he demanded.

Kelly snapped round on him.

'Keep your face shut until I speak to you,' he snarled, and then to Jimmy: 'What was the number of your seat, boy?'

'I don't know.' Jimmy avoided his eyes. 'I don't keep a check of numbers.'

'Maybe you keep a check of the play?' said Kelly. 'What was it?'

Jimmy's mind was terribly numb and dull. It groped after titles and found one.

'Eh? Well, I guess it was *The Broadway Revue* . . . yes, that's what it was.'

Kelly's underlip stuck out in contempt.

'Is that so? That happens to be the name of a picture.'

Jimmy nodded.

'Yes, that's what I saw—a picture.'

'At the Blackstone, huh?'

The boy looked round helplessly.

'Well, I don't know Chicago very well; maybe it was another theatre.'

'Can you remember the name of it?'

Behind Kelly Tony mouthed the word, almost spoke it.

'It was the Rialto,' said Jimmy.

A sardonic smile illuminated the hard face of the detective.

'Almost sounds like Blackstone, doesn't it? What time would you come out, Mr. McGrath?'

O'Hara opened his mouth to speak, but Tony silenced him with a scowl.

'What time would you leave the theatre?'

Again Jimmy sought inspiration from his chief. Tony's extended fingers rose quickly.

'Twelve, I guess.'

'Fine!' There was triumph in the word, and then, after a little pause: 'There was no performance at the Rialto last night. The projector room blew up.' Kelly beamed round at Perelli. 'Don't you guys ever read anything but the funeral notices?'

'I don't know what theatre it was,' said Jimmy sullenly, and the irrepressible Mr. O'Hara again attempted to draw the attention upon himself.

'Say, Chief, that kid's a stranger to Chicago,' he said.

He succeeded in transferring Kelly's attention to himself.

'You're an old-timer, eh?'

Con grinned.

'Why, no. I'm new on it. I'm from New York.'

Kelly shook his head.

'Never heard of the place,' he said. 'You find your way about Chicago, though.'

O'Hara smiled.

'Sure. I take a taxi.'

'Did you take a taxi to Atlantic Avenue and 95th Street last night?'

'Me? I was in bed at ten.' O'Hara was almost indignant.

'You did, though.' Kelly's accusing finger pointed at Jimmy and he came to his feet.

'No!'

'You did, too!'

'No!' This time Jimmy almost shouted the word.

With great deliberation Kelly took out a pocket-book.

'Listen: Harrigan saw Shaun before he died and he blew the works. He said he was shot by you and Con O'Hara.'

He heard a low chuckle. Tony had seated himself at his ease in one of his handsome Renaissance chairs.

'He died without speaking—I know.'

'You know, eh?'

'Sure I know,' nodded Tony. 'Why don't you arrest him?'

Perelli knew the answer to that question before Chief Kelly gave it.

'When I got him to the station house I'd find your tame lawyer with a writ of Habeas Corpus. That's why I don't arrest him,' said Kelly.

The misguided Con O'Hara intervened once more.

'Don't answer any more of his questions, kid,' he said.

'You've come to life, have you?' Kelly faced him squarely.

'Sure.'

'How long are you going to stay that way?'

'A pretty long time,' said O'Hara.

Tony had risen to his feet, was standing near the Irishman. His hand dropped quickly into O'Hara's pocket where he knew his ready gun lay and in a second it was transferred to his own.

'I'm going to stay that way a pretty long time,' repeated O'Hara.

'It'll seem long to your wife,' said Kelly, and the answer infuriated the Irishman.

He had no tact. He had dealt with policemen, had bribed them and flaunted them, and he saw no difference between Kelly and the men whom he had helped and blackmailed. What he started to say to the detective was not even printable. He had hardly uttered three words when Kelly struck him across the face with an open hand. With an oath O'Hara stepped back and dropped his hand for his gun. But the Commissioner was quicker. Like magic a thick black automatic had appeared in his hand. It rested just on the buckle of O'Hara's belt.

'Give me that rod,' he said.

He searched the Irishman scientifically.

'You haven't got one, eh? But you thought you had.'

He slipped his own into the holster under his arm, walked to where Perelli was standing, and dropped his hand almost affectionately on his shoulder.

'Perelli, I hand it to you—you're clever. The day I hang you I'm going to get drunk.' He looked at his watch and started towards the door. 'You'll be late for your appointment, Perelli. Don't keep Mike Feeney waiting.'

With this Parthian shot he left them.

'Who told him that?' O'Hara gasped, but Tony did not speak until he heard the door close on the detective. Then he rushed to the salon entrance, called Angelo and threw a command to Jimmy to get him Mike Feeney on the phone quickly. Jimmy was at the phone when Angelo entered. To him Tony gave specific instructions. There was no need to give them in detail, because Angelo had met this situation before.

By this time Feeney's call was through.

'. . . Is that you, Mike? Go steady, the wires have been tapped. . . . Kelly's been here. That's why I'm late. . . . O.K. . . . Yeh, we'll come right back. . . . All right, Mike.'

He hung up the receiver.

Angelo came running in with his overcoat and hat.

'Got the boys outside? Fine. You come along, Con.' He looked at Jimmy thoughtfully. 'No, Jimmy, you stay here. I'll be back in a few minutes.' He turned to Angelo. 'Angelo, you go over to Schoberg's.'

Angelo had already been 'over to Schoberg's'. That also was part of the routine of a gang killing, and to Schoberg he had handed a black-edged card on which, legibly inscribed, was a poem. Angelo was something of a versifier and had composed many obituary pieces.

Over the phone Mike Feeney had conveyed the bright thought which explained his readiness to meet his enemy. It had occurred instantly also to Tony Perelli. This was to be no secret meeting between gang chiefs; rather a meeting, if not under the auspices, certainly under the surveillance of the Police Department. So there would be no shooting on either side. If the police knew of the conference—as evidently they did—any breach of the common law would be fraught with danger to both parties.

Tony had not reached the rendezvous when he realised that his own view and Mike Feeney's warning were justified. There were squad cars at the corner of every block. The avenue was alive with men from the Central Detective Bureau. When they met and shook hands like respectable citizens they did so in the presence of a cloud of witnesses, and Mike Feeney was conscious of his audience.

His gunmen had melted away, but were within hail. So too had Tony's.

' 'Lo, Mike!' was Tony's commonplace greeting.

They gripped hands without fear one of the other.

'You come back to my apartment, Mike?' asked Perelli.

Big Mike looked sideways, seeking support.

'Them boys can follow in,' said Tony. 'We don't want no trouble. That's Kelly's car just went past. Say, Mike, that guy is like a brother to you.'

Mike hesitated. He was unusually nervous, for somewhere in the background was his sister. In this car or that which went speeding past she might be sitting—and she could work a machine-gun as well as any man. Hating Tony as she did, hating him with malignity beyond his own understanding—there was reason for his nervousness.

'Sure, I'll go with you,' he said.

They went up together in Tony's big elevator, which was kept exclusively for his use when he was in the building. He let himself into his apartment and was a most willing witness of the climax of the little idyll which had followed his exit.

8

Jimmy heard the door close on his master; sat with his head in his hands, thinking, wondering. . . . In his soul was a whirl of confused fear and resentment. He might get out of Chicago, but he would carry his burden with him, a burden of guilt, of treachery. His was the guilt of Cain. There was no place to go to. . . .

If he could have walked into Kelly's office and confessed his crime without involving Con O'Hara and Perelli he would have accepted that as a solution of his tremendous problem. If he could go out into a new, clean world . . . But he would carry his world with him wherever he went and for all time.

Jimmy McGrath knew there was only one way out. By his own hand? No! That would be cheating. His life was forfeit. He must pay his debt to his real creditors.

'What is the matter, Jimmy?'

He looked up quickly. Minn Lee was standing within a foot of him, so serene, so calm, so radiant in an unearthly way that the sight of her caught his breath.

'Hallo, Minn Lee,' his voice quivered.

'What's wrong, Jimmy? Aren't you well?'

He shook his head. Again his face dropped into his hands. 'No. . . .' A long pause. 'I wish I were dead!'

She sat down by his side and laid her little hand on his knee. In her voice was a note of gentle reproach.

'Oh, Jimmy, I told you to go away,' she said sadly.

He sat upright, looked at her and laughed.

'Go away—where?'

She sighed, and he looked at her pityingly.

'I wish you weren't in this,' he said.

She looked up.

112

'In the racket,' he explained. 'Can't you get out? You have no business here.'

Minn Lee picked up her embroidery frame and surveyed it for a long time in silence.

'My business is every woman's business, Jimmy. When you're in it, you're in it for life,' she said.

He could only wonder at her as he had wondered before. Was she what she seemed to him or what she seemed to Tony Perelli? Was his idealism a flimsy structure based on illusion?

'Doesn't it make a difference to you—these rackets and murders?'

She shrugged.

'No. If Tony were a stockholder it would be no different for me.'

And then he asked her a question he meant to have asked her before.

'You must have gone to a good school, Minn Lee. You talk somehow—well, like somebody . . .'

'I went to Columbia.'

'University? Gee! Did you get a degree?'

She nodded.

'Well, how in the name of Mike did you get here?'

She didn't look up from her work.

'Well, you know,' she said vaguely. 'Art, love, not knowing what to do about it. There it is!'

He felt towards her an infinite tenderness, would have given his life, if it were not already forfeited, to get her out of the place. He said as much.

'Get yourself out,' she said. 'Soon.'

He shook his head. He was in for life, too, until the end of life.

He rose and paced up and down the room, thinking she was still absorbed in her work, but when he turned his head he saw her surveying him with a little puzzled frown.

'Jimmy. . . . Who killed that man last night?'

The question was a shocking one. For the moment he had forgotten Shaun O'Donnell.

'I . . . I don't know,' he said unsteadily.

'Who killed him?' she asked again.

And then something inside him snapped and he was down

on his knees by her side, his face buried in her lap. Jimmy McGrath had indeed fallen apart.

'I did it, Minn Lee, I did it,' he sobbed. 'I tried to get drunk to do it—and with every drink I got more and more sober. I killed him. I killed him in cold blood. I've got to pay—I know that. But I want to pay soon—I want it to come soon—now!'

She nodded.

'It will come very soon for you—and for me,' she said.

'For you?' He looked up, saw the blurred image of her through his streaming eyes. 'Nobody would hurt you.'

And then he realised that she was being hurt all the time, hurt by Perelli, hurt by him, that she was not the unemotional, philosophical Easterner at all, that the fifty per cent American in her was there to feel and to suffer. He groped for her hand and caught it.

'I love you, Minn Lee,' he whispered. 'There's nothing worth while but you. I haven't said this before to anybody.'

She freed her hand.

'I have nothing to give you, nothing,' she said. Her voice was level, almost monotonous. 'I am waste, no good for anybody'

And then he began to blurt wild plans, conceived in that moment, that they should go away, get across to Canada, go beyond Perelli's discovery, where neither he nor his gang could trace them.

She brought him to his senses with a little laugh.

'A Chinese girl and a boy! Jimmy, no! I have nothing to give. My body belongs here—to Tony. I want no other man. I have not enough to give him—I love him so.'

'Other women have lived in this apartment.' The desire for her drove him to disloyalty.

She knew that.

'And they have gone—you know where?'

She knew but she was not afraid.

She tried to bring him to sanity. Tony would be good to him, she thought, if he would stay. He loved her, that was all he knew. He repeated this. Again she shook her head.

'I love only Tony.'

Tony Perelli, standing in the doorway, saw this, beamed

114

upon them as a benevolent father might beam upon his children.

Jimmy heard his murmur and scrambled to his feet, but Tony arrested his babbling apology.

'Ah, Jimmy, no. You are not to feel damn' foolish. It was so nize. Run away now, you two little babies. Take him up to your apartment, my pretty flower.'

Again Jimmy tried to speak, but was shooed away. Tony's smile was benign—mechanically benign.

He watched the two until they passed out of sight; still stood staring after them for a long time.

Mike Feeney came into the salon fearfully. It was not his first visit, but many things had happened since he was here last. Vinsetti, for example—the peculiar circumstances of his passing had been a nine-days' wonder in the world of gangdom. A place of death, this, for all the masses of blooms that frothed in blue Ming vases, for all the austerity of the organ and the faint fragrance of burning joss-sticks.

He turned at the door and addressed his followers loudly, rather to encourage himself with the knowledge of their support than to offer them instructions.

'You guys, park your guns. That's the arrangement, ain't it, Tony?'

Tony understood and smiled.

'Sure thing. Lay your guns on the table and help yourselves to a drink.'

Feeney pulled two guns from the holsters strapped under his arms and laid them on the table with a flourish.

'There's mine,' he said.

Tony drew guns from the specially tailored pockets on his hips and put them by the side of the other weapons.

'Where's Angelo?' Mike looked round.

'I sent him down to Schoberg's,' said Tony significantly. Mike was pleased.

'Sure, that's a grand idea! You're a wonderful guy for thinking up notions,' he conceded handsomely. 'The boys will be pleased at that.'

Tony opened a drawer in the table with a bang that brought his guest spinning round apprehensively. But it was a familiar box that Perelli produced and opened.

'Have a cigar?'

115

Mike selected one.

'I don't smoke as a rule. It's bad for the eyes.'

Neither of the men saw Minn Lee as she crossed the balcony. There was a stone canopy which acted as a sounding board. One could stand out of sight and hear the lowest-toned conversation: she had discovered this the day she had arrived at the apartment. Tony had never made the discovery because he rarely went to the balcony unless the salon was empty. One Angelo Beratachi was shot dead on the third-floor balcony of his flat by an enemy who opened fire on him from another balcony five hundred yards away. Gangsters never take the same risk twice.

'Now see here, Mike.' Tony lit a cigar. 'What I said over the wire goes. We are both making money. For a few dollars one way or the other why all this trouble?'

'Ain't that right?' Feeney's enthusiasm was a little forced. 'I've always said you have more under your hat than any college professor.'

Perelli drew two chairs to the centre of the room and they sat knee to knee.

'But, Tony, I'm giving you this straight: I've got a pretty tough lot of hoodlums, and half the trouble is Shaun.'

Tony murmured something, and the other man raised a protesting hand.

'I know, I know. Shaun didn't like you. He went after you, and I might have done the same, but I've got a sister who married him. Well, you know what women are. She's out to get the birds that got her man, and the gang is with her.'

'Your sister,' said Perelli politely, 'is a very nize woman.'

But Mike had no illusions.

'She's not your kind, Perelli. She never had no sex appeal for anybody except Shaun. And that's the trouble.'

Tony came straight to the point.

'What do you want me to do?'

Leaning forward, Mike spoke deliberately.

'We know the guys that got Shaun—that kid McGrath and Con O'Hara. One of my boys saw them smoking back to the city. That kid's yellow, too. I'm sorry for Con—I knew him in New York—but he's certainly a loud noise. Seen his woman?'

Tony had seen his woman—and had not forgotten her.

116

'Yes, I have seen his woman. What do you want me to do?' he asked again.

Mike Feeney lowered his voice.

'Put them on the spot tonight. Eleven o'clock at the corner of Michigan and Ninety-fourth. I'll have a couple of boys there and that'll finish it.'

'I wouldn't do that to a yellow dog,' said Tony hotly.

'I respect you for it, but . . .'

Perelli laid his chin in his chubby fist.

'These guys are certainly a whole lot of trouble to me,' he said, and at the sign of his weakening Mike's spirits rose.

'There's yeller guys in every outfit—remember Vinsetti?'

'I knew him . . .'

Feeney smiled grimly.

'He was yeller—tried to take a powder on you, didn't he?'

'He was talking of quitting,' said Perelli indifferently.

'He came to this apartment and was never seen no more till they picked him up on Lake Shore.' Mike was impressively dramatic.

'I read about it,' said Tony. 'I don't want no trouble,' he went on slowly. 'O.K., I'll put them on the spot.'

They got to their feet together as a knock came at the door. It was Angelo. They did not see him at first, because he was hidden behind a great floral harp which he carried forward with stately tread and deposited before the men.

A beautiful harp. One of Schoberg's grandest efforts—and Schoberg was the swellest florist in Chicago. Mike Feeney was touched.

'That's mighty thoughtful. Gee, I appreciate that.'

He lifted the black-bordered card and read:

> The Angels heard the voice of Shaun
> And said: 'Another good man gone.'
>
> Deepest sympathy from Tony Perelli.

Mike's voice broke. 'Jeez! That's lovely!' he wailed.

Tony's parties were always swell. This wildly extemporised party of his might have been justified by some outstanding achievement.

Not a tactful party, with Shaun O'Donnell resting under

earth and the weight of truck loads of flowers. It was bad luck for Shaun that the bishop refused him burial in consecrated ground. His shrill wife protested violently. There were actually cables despatched to the Holy See, but nothing came of that. In the unblessed ground he lay for at least a month. Then loyal hands dug him up and laid him at the very feet of the bishop's predecessor.

For the moment here he was—'and in hell, I have no doubt,' said Monseigneur irritably—in a corner of the Baptists' lot. And in consequence a big party would be unseemly.

But a party of sorts was necessary to Perelli; here was a moment which called for wine and trumpets. These were proper accessories to a grand going out from life of beloved enemies. Wine was part of the ritual of destruction. There was a certain society in Chicago that had its killings. The members of the society were fellow countrymen of Tony's. And always, when the police came running at the sound of shots and forced the door of an apartment to find a sprawled, bloody-faced thing on the floor, there on the near-by table they would find the bottles and the used glasses—generally there were three—of killer and killed.

When the boys and the girls were dancing, Tony beckoned his lieutenant into the salon.

'Listen, Angelo, I'm sending Con and Jimmy up on the West Side.'

He said this carelessly. At first Angelo did not comprehend.

'Oh yeh?' Then, quickly: 'What's the idea?'

Too well he knew the idea.

'O'Hara's shooting out of his mouth,' said Tony.

He tried to throw a note of regret into his voice and failed. Angelo, staring at him, nodded.

'Yeh, he's better dumb. He's only a big noise. But the kid . . .'

He frowned, which was not like Angelo. He was not so much shocked as puzzled. Why Jimmy? He asked the question in those words.

'You saw him? He fell apart. If Kelly ever gets him to headquarters . . .'

Perelli for once failed to convince his shadow.

118

'Of course he fell apart.' Angelo's voice was silky. 'Didn't I tell you not to send him? He might have been useful. He could still be useful.'

He saw Tony's eyes wander to the balcony. Minn Lee was there. Angelo frowned. Not because of Minn Lee, surely? That was outside of business—a reprehensible motive.

The girl came down and stood watching silently. Angelo, sensing the tension, was glad to make his escape.

There was a certain odd doubt in Perelli's mind—a suspicion that was instinctive. He had missed Minn Lee; even in the wild excitement of Maria's association he had missed her.

'Where have you been all the night?' he asked.

She looked him straight in the eyes.

'In my room,' she said.

'When I have a party you go to your room! And has Jimmy McGrath been in your room, too?'

The answer came with shocking unexpectedness.

'Yes.'

He stared at her. She could not have been in her room all the night. He had gone to her apartment and found the door locked. She only turned the key when she was out.

'I suppose you and Jimmy were in the room when the door was locked?'

'Yes.'

He drew a long, whistling breath.

'Ain't you got the nerve!'

He could hardly speak the words. She and Jimmy in her room . . . and the door was locked.

'You told me to get him away from the party.' There was a half-smile on the curved red lips. 'Well . . . I got him away from the party!'

'Sure I told you,' he said huskily; and then, as the enormity of her offence took a clear appearance, he gripped her by the arm. 'But did I tell you to stay with him in your room and lock the door?'

She did not wince, gave no sign of the pain she felt when his powerful hand pressed the bracelet into her flesh. Nor, under his furious gaze, did she flinch. With a jerk of his hand he released her.

'Where are all the pretty ladies and gentlemen?' he asked.

He was not interested in the pretty ladies and gentlemen: only in her and in Jimmy and the significance of the fastened door.

'In the Winter Garden—they are dancing.'

'You locked the door—huh? I asked the question for a joke. Could I imagine you'd say "Yes"?' He took control of himself. 'Tell Jimmy I want him.'

For the first time she showed alarm.

'Are you going to say anything to Jimmy? It was my fault.'

He shook his head.

'No, ao, no. Jimmy is a nize feller. I am fond of Jimmy.' He looked at his watch. 'You go tell him I want to see him.'

As she walked to the door:

'Oh, Minn Lee. I want Con O'Hara, too. . . . Come here.'

Obediently she returned. Knowing him so well, she was not surprised when he slipped his arm around her shoulder.

'Don't take notice of me. I am worried with business. Don't be . . .' His gesture was expressive. 'You know? And, Minn Lee—you look after Mrs. O'Hara, eh? She's a swell woman, but she's not in your street, Minn Lee. If Con asks anything, say you're looking after her. Tell her what a swell feller I am. Didn't I send you to the coast, and give you a house, and dress you up so as to make these dames in Hollywood look like 'ired 'elps?'

She drew away from him. 'You can tell her that,' she said.

Again he looked at his watch.

'Go get those boys. Why did you lock the door?'

That was at the back of his mind.

'I didn't want anybody to come in,' she said simply, and his lips curled.

'Crying or somep'n'? Phew! If Kelly ever gets that kid down to headquarters there'll be hell to pay . . .'

Minn Lee was smiling.

'He wasn't crying,' she said.

When the door closed behind her he sat down on the settle near the big table, biting thoughtfully at his nails. Minn Lee had suddenly become the most incomprehensible person. This was not the Minn Lee he knew, the obedient slave to his whims. Of a sudden she had assumed a disconcerting independence.

His thoughts were interrupted by the ringing of the telephone. He took up the receiver, and knew it was Mike Feeney before he heard the harsh voice of the man.

Mike was apprehensive, a little fretful. Tony sensed behind all this the urgent nagging of the man's bony sister.

Say, did Tony know what the time was? And was there any change of plan? His boys wanted to know this, his boys wanted to know that. It did not make it any easier for Tony Perelli to know that 'his boys' was Mrs. O'Donnell.

'Don't push me around, Mike,' he said angrily. 'I said eleven; it's a quarter off . . . that's all right. They can make it in ten minutes. Only don't start pushing me around, that's all. When I give my word . . .'

Out of the corner of his eye he saw the door open and Jimmy come in. He ended the conversation abruptly, hung up the receiver, and greeted Jimmy with a smile.

'Sorry I'm breaking up the party for you, Jimmy boy. You know Captain Strude?'

Jimmy shook his head.

'A police captain?'

'No,' smiled Jimmy, 'I don't know any police captains in Chicago.'

'That's O.K.,' said Tony. 'We call him "Lefty", and that's the name he'll be calling himself tonight.'

'You want me to find him . . .'

'He'll find you—and don't let that scare you.'

He looked the boy up and down admiringly.

'You're looking grand tonight,' he said, and beckoned him to a seat on the settle beside him. 'Laughing, too! Ain't you the great boy! Why, you're so different to what you was this morning.'

The change in Jimmy was obvious; his eye was brighter, the old depression had left him, and he carried himself almost jauntily. A good-looking boy, thought Tony Perelli dispassionately; a boy who could wear swell clothes and never look like a waiter.

'I guess I'm feeling better,' said Jimmy.

Tony nodded.

'That lousy copper got your goat. Say, he's nothing,' he said contemptuously.

'Mr. Kelly?'

Tony waggled his head impatiently.

'Ah, don't call him mister—he ain't here.'

Jimmy was whistling softly, only interrupting the tune to speak. He was whistling now as he examined his hands—those guilty hands of his.

'That's a tough job,' he said. 'I hated Kelly this morning; now I've got a sort of sympathetic feeling towards him.'

'Don't be too sympathetic,' said Tony quickly. 'Sympathy's a bad thing to have in our business, Jimmy. You're sympathetic with Minn Lee, ain't you?'

He asked the question carelessly, and had the answer he least expected.

'Yes,' said Jimmy quietly. 'I love her.'

Tony twisted round in his seat to see the boy better. He was searching his face.

'Yeh? Love her, eh? She's swell. I've made her.'

He dusted an invisible speck of fluff from his sleeve.

'Everything she owes to me. She was living with a painter fellow when I found her . . .'

'Does it matter?'

'To me, no. I'm broad-minded. What is an artist—nothing. Hardly a human being.'

Here came Con, brusque, very confident, hiding with more skill than usual his resentment against his employer. And he had cause for resentment, for he had been a watchful, jealous man that night.

'Oh, Con, do you know Lefty Strude, the police captain?'

'No, I don't know any of these guys, but believe me, I won't be here in Chicago long before I do.'

'Sure you won't.'

Tony got up and, going to the other side of the table, opened a drawer, took out an envelope, and laid it on the table.

'You take that, Jimmy; put it in your pocket, and be careful—there's thirty thousand dollars in that cover. I've got a cargo of liquor coming through the Erie Canal. That's nothing to do with you, boy. You take this letter to the corner of Michigan and Ninety-fourth. Strude will drive up in his car round about eleven. He'll say "Lefty"—and that's all. Hand him the letter and get right back. You ought be here by a quarter after eleven.'

O'Hara watched the envelope disappear into Jimmy's pocket, and a deep frown furrowed his face.

'Say, what's the idea of sending me?' he demanded. 'You don't want two of us to carry a letter, do you?'

'That's not too many to look after thirty thousand dollars,' said Tony. 'I'm not trusting Mike farther than I can throw him. He knows the money is going forward tonight.'

Con looked at him suspiciously. He got up and was half-way to the door before Tony realised that he was leaving.

'What's the idea?' he demanded.

'I'm going to call Mrs. O'Hara and leave her at my apartment.'

Tony smiled.

'Leave Mrs. O'Hara at your apartment? What's the big idea? She's staying the night—and you also. I have rooms for you.'

As Con O'Hara opened the door the woman they were discussing came in. She was curious to know what was going forward. Con had been sent for, and there must be a reason for that. He had been nagging her into leaving all the evening. It was like Con to try to spoil her party.

'I'm taking you home, and I'm picking you up on my way back,' said Con, and she stared at him.

'What the hell am I?' she asked. 'Something you bought at Marshall Field's? Where are you going, anyway?'

Tony smiled at her.

'That's the one question you must never ask.'

She looked from one to the other, and her eye rested for a moment on Jimmy.

'Is he going too? It ain't one of these stick-up jobs, is it?'

Perelli's expression was pained.

'No, no, no! Don't think of such things.'

Jimmy watched the scene not without amusement. He offered a suggestion which was partly mischievous, partly serious.

'I'll go alone. I guess I can look after myself,' he said—a solution which was very agreeable to O'Hara.

'Sure you can . . .' he began, but Tony turned round on him with a snarl.

'What's all this? Do I ask you to pick and choose what you shall do and what you shall not do?' he demanded.

'Are you so yellow that you're afraid to go with this boy? If there was any danger should I send Jimmy, who is like my own brother?'

The man cringed before him, and that was not like Con.

'O.K.,' he said loudly. 'I'll get my coat.'

He caught his wife's eyes and held them.

'Mrs. Perelli's looking after you, kid. You understand?'

'Who's been telling you I want a chaperon?' she grumbled.

'You've said it!' chuckled Tony. 'So long, Jimmy! Come back soon.'

Then he saw something in the boy's waistcoat pocket— the upper half of a silver cigarette-case. His stubby fore-finger went out and tapped it.

'Say, what's that?'

Jimmy looked down.

'That's a cigarette-case,' said Jimmy. 'My—well, some-body gave it to me.'

Tony nodded. His sly eyes looked smilingly up at Jimmy's.

'Somebody nize, eh? You wear it over your 'eart?'

'It happens to be there.'

Tony shook his head.

'I wouldn't keep it there, Jimmy. Put it on your hip. It don't look good.'

For a moment Jimmy was puzzled and then, in a flash, understanding came to him. He took the cigarette-case slowly from his waistcoat and dropped it into his hip pocket.

'Why, of course! It would be in the way, wouldn't it?'

The smile went out of Perelli's face. The boy had said something brutally true. What did he know? He must know something, suspect something. And if he did know, who could have told him?

From the salon a short, broad corridor led to the hall. Jimmy was half-way down this when he heard a voice be-hind him, and turned to meet Minn Lee running towards him. He held out his arms; she came into them, and for a moment he held her. She was oblivious of Tony Perelli, standing at the door, watching them, open-mouthed; of

124

Maria, amused and a little shocked, for women of the Maria class have their conventions.

'You were going without saying good-bye, Jimmy,' she said breathlessly. 'Are you happy?'

He nodded.

'By God, I am!' he said in a low voice. 'You don't know how happy!'

She lifted her face to his and, stooping, he kissed her. In another second he had joined Con O'Hara, who was waiting at the open elevator door, grumbling loudly at the task he had been given.

Minn Lee came straight back to the salon. She saw neither Perelli nor the woman who was to supplant her; she stared ahead into infinity, was conscious only of those tremendous things which were in her mind and in her heart. Perelli spoke to her, but she did not answer. She had one wish, entirely selfish, it was that Jimmy should think well of her; she wanted nothing more than that. She was moving in a haze of wonder—of accomplishment.

'Hey, do you hear me?'

She heard Tony's roar and turned a smiling face to him. How big and grand and powerful he was, and yet . . .

'You come up and dance with me, Tony?' she said gaily. 'I will be the prettiest woman in the room. Jimmy said so.'

Tony Perelli stood stock still in the centre of the room after she had gone. She would be the prettiest woman in the room—Jimmy said so. He was hurt, terribly hurt; and yet he had already decided the fate of Minn Lee, had arranged that very day to send her away to a new and ugly life. He had sent women before. He was finished and done with her, as he had been finished and done with other lights of love, and thought no more of them. Even in the height of their favour they meant little to him, no more than the furniture or the decorations of the apartment, as he had told her. But she could still hurt him: that was the painful discovery he made, a new experience, a tremendous thing, almost unendurable.

He heard Maria's taunting little laugh, but still he stood, gazing blankly at the door through which she had passed. Presently he found his voice.

'She locked the door,' he said slowly.

'For God's sake! She's got a sweetie,' crooned Maria archly. 'I like that kid.'

And then her mind went back to more important matters.

'Where are those two gone?' she asked.

He made no reply.

'Con and Jimmy McGrath,' she said impatiently. 'Mr. Tony Perelli, are you dumb?'

He was neither dumb nor deaf, but his mind was completely occupied by the staggering phenomenon he had witnessed.

'She didn't say "yes",' he said slowly, 'and she didn't say "no"—she just side-stepped it. . . . She'll be the prettiest woman in the room—Jimmy says so!'

The smile left her face, and the hard mouth grew harder.

'Are you going to dance or just talk to yourself all night? How long will Con be away?'

Tony came back with a start to another reality. Con was gone; that was the end of him. He laughed in her face.

'He'll be away just long enough,' he said, and put his arm about her.

She struggled free.

'You're damned sure, aren't you? Come and dance.'

But he led her to the big settee and pushed her down.

'Don't go up there with all that bunch,' he pleaded. 'Sit right here. Nobody's coming in.'

He drew her towards him and kissed her, and she offered no more than the amount of resistance which the situation demanded. She was conventional, inclined towards respectability, or at any rate worshipped the respectable appearances of life.

'You've got mean ideas about yourself, haven't you?' She pushed him away from her and looked at him. 'Suppose somebody came in—your wife?'

All the light went out of his eyes, and again she stared into two dead pools. Angrily she rose to her feet.

'Oh, hell! If you're going blah on me I'll get another partner,' she said.

He tried to catch her arm but she wrenched it free. He followed her into the ballroom and rescued her from the partner who came to claim her.

126

9

One thing was sure, grumbled Con: that Tony Perelli was
a bad timer. There was a time for business and a time for
pleasure, and it was against all the rules and traditions to
mix 'em. What was the matter with coppers, anyway, that
they couldn't step right up in daylight and take their cut?
If any investigating committee of the Clean Police movement went after 'em, hadn't they banking accounts to be
examined, and did it matter whether they took their wages
on the corner of the deserted streets or through an open
cheque, so long as it was there and could not be accounted
for except by crooked dealing?

Jimmy was driving the coupé. There were no nerves
about him tonight.

Con noted this with interest. He had seen such unbe-
lievable changes come to men before, but he had never
expected to see the phenomenon in Jimmy.

'What did Kelly want to see Perelli for?' he asked suddenly.

'Kelly?'

Con nodded.

'Yeah. He went into the building just as you came out.
I thought you'd meet him.'

Jimmy did not answer.

The green light before him went suddenly red and he
stopped the car at the traffic signal.

'How do you find life, Con?' he asked.

Con turned his head to look at him in amazement.

'How's that?' he asked.

'How do you find the world? Does it use you well? Would
you like to go on being in it with your—wife, and everything?'

Con O'Hara grinned.

'Sure. That's how I'm going to be,' he said.

'And that's why I'm dropping you just short of our rendezvous.'

Con made a grumbling noise of enquiry.

'The place where we're meeting this police captain,' explained Jimmy. 'I guess I'd better go on alone. You take the wheel and I'll get ready to jump.'

O'Hara swung round in his seat.

'What's the big idea?' he asked slowly.

'Do you know what being put on the spot means?' asked Jimmy.

'Sure I know.'

There was a little silence.

The red light went to green and the car moved forward, going faster.

'It's funny,' said Jimmy. He was talking half to himself and half to his companion. 'I didn't realise what it meant until today. It comes from the pictures they publish in newspapers, doesn't it? The cross marks the spot where the body was found, when they put you on the spot. The figure is washed out for fear of hurting the feelings of sensitive people and a big cross is put in its place.'

'Who's being put on the spot?' asked Con deliberately.

He heard a little sigh.

'I guess we are,' said Jimmy. 'At least, I am. I'm dropping you, or, rather, you're dropping me.' He thought for a while. 'No, I guess I'd better drop you. If they don't see the car they'll think Perelli has double-crossed them . . .'

'Say, listen, give me this so's I can get it, will ya? Are we being put on the spot . . . ? Is that dirty Sicilian . . . ?'

'I think so,' said Jimmy gravely. 'I don't know why he wants you to go out, but he certainly wants me.'

Con O'Hara was breathing quickly.

'Who told you this?'

In the darkness Jimmy smiled.

'Somebody who wouldn't tell me a lie.'

'Minn Lee?'

'Somebody who wouldn't tell me a lie,' repeated Jimmy. 'I guess I'd better drop you here.'

He drew the car up to the sidewalk.

'You're crazy,' said Con. 'If that's true, what's the idea of you going on? Want to be put on the spot?'

Jimmy McGrath did not answer, and a suspicion crossed the dull mind of the man by his side.

'You making a getaway with all that money in your pocket?' he asked.

Jimmy switched on the light on the dash-board and took the envelope from his pocket; without hesitation he thumbed open the flap of the cover, and drew out a thick pad of blank sheets of paper. 'All that money,' he said mockingly. 'That would keep me in luxury for the rest of my life!'

Con O'Hara snatched the paper from him, turned sheet after sheet and gasped.

'It's not money . . . just paper!' he breathed.

'Will you get down?'

Jimmy leaned across him and pushed open the door. Only for a second did Con O'Hara hesitate. He looked along the dark thoroughfare. There was nobody in sight. Near at hand he saw an avenue of escape, a narrow passage between two high-standing tenement houses.

'I'll watch you,' he said breathlessly. 'You go on, Jimmy. . . . Got a gun?'

Jimmy shook his head.

'I don't want a gun.'

He pulled the door of the coupé closed and with a wave of his hand went on.

He came to the appointed place, stopped the car and got out. There was nobody in sight. Then the lights of a car came into view. Moving swiftly, it passed him with a roar. Nobody in sight. . . . Yes, there was another car, moving more slowly and hugging the edge of the sidewalk. Nearer and nearer. . . . A closed roadster. . . .

A few yards from him the leather curtains at the side moved. . . .

Jimmy McGrath drew himself up stiffly. He must have seen the flicker-flicker of flame as the machine-gun opened fire. He could have felt nothing. . . .

Down on the sidewalk he fell, an inert heap. He had paid as he had expected to pay.

Reporters would be flocking here in less than an hour,

pictures would cover the front pages of the Chicago press, and a cross would mark the spot where the account of Shaun O'Donnell was half settled.

It was Angelo who admitted the Chief of Detectives, and if he showed some apprehension it was only natural, for Angelo had the clearest vision of all gangsters, and recognised the potential danger represented by this hard-faced man.

Between Kelly and him there was a sort of sympathy which was difficult to define. Kelly had marked Angelo as the future leader of the gang which Perelli controlled, and he saw that there would not only be a change in methods, but a considerable improvement in the state of affairs, when the time came for Angelo to take charge.

'Where's Perelli?' he asked roughly.

Looking around, he saw the empty champagne bottles and glasses, and even without the strains of music would have known there was a party in progress.

'He's just stepped out to see a friend,' said Angelo quickly.

Kelly smiled.

'He doesn't step out to see anybody without his armoured car, and that hasn't left the garage.'

Angelo accepted the rebuff. He was not abashed: it was part of his duty to lie.

He grew confidential.

'He's gone up to the ballroom,' he said, 'with a dame, and that's the truth. You know what Tony is with a skirt! Have a drink, Chief? I'll get him down.'

Kelly walked up and down the apartment.

'Mike Feeney was around here today,' he said.

Angelo nodded.

'Mike an' us is like brothers,' he said.

Kelly showed his teeth.

'Yuh—like Cain and Abel,' he said. 'Where's that boy McGrath? Is he a brother?'

Angelo smiled sweetly.

'He's around. Nice kid that, Chief.'

'Around where? I saw him at the door as I came in. Find Perelli—I want to see him.'

Angelo went to the door as Kelly asked:

'What's the idea of the party?'

'We've only got a little one up in the Winter Garden,' said Angelo with an apologetic smile. 'Tony thought it wouldn't be right, him an' Mike being good frien's, to throw a big party tonight. Shaun was buried this afternoon. Say, there was no flowers! None at all! Only eight truck-loads! Shaun looked grand, all done up in a silver casket—cost seven grand. There must have been five thousand dollars worth of flowers—think of it, Chief. Five grand wasted on damn' lilies! All that money could have gone to us poor!'

As Angelo left Minn Lee came in and went to her favourite seat on the couch. She had an embroidery frame in her hand, and evidently she had no particular interest in the party.

Kelly greeted her with a friendly nod.

'All dressed up, Minn Lee?' he asked.

She looked lovely in a gold dress that fitted her like a glove. Usually she wore a Chinese costume, but tonight she was a Westerner, and the golden sheen of her Paris frock blended with the ivory tint of her lovely skin.

She looked down at her dress with a smile, and then up at the Commissioner.

'Yes—is it pretty?'

'Grand,' said Kelly, sardonically, but she accepted his words literally and for the first time he heard her laugh.

He was watching her with a puzzled frown.

'I've never seen you looking so cheerful, Minn Lee,' he said. 'Say, I dreamt about you the other night.'

She raised her eyebrows.

'Oh, Mr. Kelly! I thought you dreamt only of prisons and ropes and gunmen!'

He chuckled at this.

'Well, you're on my mind, young woman; I've got a kind of nice feeling about you, and that's a fact.'

'Have you?' she said with a touch of coquetry. 'This is my lucky day!'

'That doesn't mean I want to call on you when Tony's out,' said Kelly. 'Don't tell me you're disappointed, because I know you're not. The fact is, Minn Lee, that in spite of all your peculiar and unfortunate adventures in

131

this love world of yours, I have a remarkable respect for you. You're the only real person in this place.'

He sneered up at the painted ceiling.

'You don't belong to this, and that's a fact. There's nothing in this room that isn't an imitation of something else. The apartment is copied from something in Venice, the pictures are copies of something in Rome, and the furniture is true-to-life models from Verona.'

She was amused.

'Art was my downfall,' she said lightly. 'And am I a replica of something somewhere?'

'You're real,' he nodded, and then, with a cautious look round, he asked: 'When are you leaving?'

'Who told you I was leaving?' she asked quickly.

So she knew, or guessed, he thought.

'You're about due for a move,' he said. 'I've seen three girls sitting in this apartment and looking like a million dollars, and I've seen 'em go.'

She nodded.

'I know. Poor girls!'

In her voice was a note of carelessness.

'Perhaps you know how your man got the money to make all this whoopee?' he asked.

She lifted her shoulder slightly.

'Booze,' she said.

'Yuh, booze,' repeated Kelly, 'and with something else. He's got three houses at Cicero and two at Burnham—forty girls in each house. Two thousand dollars profit every night—two grand a night out of women!'

Her hands were folded on her lap. She did not look at him.

'Yes, I know,' she said in a low voice. 'I am not a child. Of course I know. Why do you tell me?'

There was a reason why he should tell her. She was to hear something that was to fill her with panic, though she showed no visible sign of this.

'The head girl at the swell house at Cicero is in bad with Perelli,' he said. 'She's been snitching money. Somebody's going to take her place.'

The panic passed. She did not care really. He sensed her reaction and wondered.

'That doesn't mean anything to me,' she said. 'You should have told me yesterday, then I would have been sad. Today nothing will hurt me—nothing. What time is it?'

A silvery-toned clock was striking somewhere.

Kelly looked at his watch.

'Eleven. Why?'

A look of ecstasy came to her face. Had he imagined that her cheeks had gone a little paler? There was something in her eyes he had never seen before. He stared at her in wonder. She was gazing into vacancy.

'Eleven!'

He hardly heard the whispered word.

'That's nice . . . !'

'Why, Minn Lee, what the mischief's wrong with you?'

'Don't talk for a little minute!'

Her eyes were closed, her hands clasped over the heaving little breast. She looked like some ecstatic deity in the fervour of her devotion.

'Why, Minn Lee, you look like the Queen of China!' he said admiringly.

Her hand shot out.

'Kiss my hand,' she said imperiously. 'I am a queen this minute . . . queen of myself . . . ! I think for the first time in my life!'

He was holding her hand, on which a great diamond glistened. He looked at the ring curiously, fingering the stone.

'That's a grand sparkler of yours, Minn Lee.'

She nodded. Her mind and heart were elsewhere at that moment. He would have been shocked had he known where.

'I've seen it before,' he went on. 'Every girl who has lived here has worn it.'

She came back to consciousness with a little smile and a sigh.

'Yes, I suppose so.'

'One day Perelli will tell you that he wants it and you'll give it to him and you'll never see it again.'

She looked at the ring curiously as though she had never seen it before.

133

'I don't want it—what is it? It means nothing to me,' she said.

'Some day he'll send you out to Cicero,' he said deliberately. 'You know what you'll do there?'

She shook her head.

'You'll take charge of the big house where the swell fellows go.'

'No!'

The word came vehemently, passionately. For a moment he thought he had shocked her.

'And then, after a year,' he continued, 'you'll go down to the second house, where they drink beer and bad hooch, and then, by and by, you'll have a room in the third house, where there's no colour bar.'

'No!'

He swung her round by the shoulders and looked down into her face.

'That's the way the others went, Minn Lee. All of them. Every girl who's been "Mrs. Perelli" has ended her career in the same racket.'

A long pause.

'I can see a way out for you, kid.'

She also could see a way out—the best way of all, but he did not know this. His mind was intent only on the trapping of Perelli.

'There's a hundred thousand dollars unclaimed reward for the Vinsetti murder. The money's deposited at the Union Bank. Tony Perelli did that—solo. You know it.'

She made a little gesture of despair and sat down in one of the high-backed Renaissance chairs.

'I thought you were going to be so interesting,' she said, 'and you aren't. You are just being a policeman, and I like you so much better when you're human.'

Kelly looked round and lowered his voice. He knew all that had been happening in this house—everything. He knew better than she how far Tony Perelli was compromised with the wife of Con O'Hara. He had a record of Maria that was most definite and unpleasant. Also she had a girl friend in Chicago and had talked boastfully of the great future which was hers. Women talk to women, and they talk to men. Eventually police headquarters lends a listening ear.

This was the moment to catch her on the rebound. She must know about Maria, and if she did . . .

'You've nothing to be afraid of—none of the gangs would touch you. The only thing we hang 'em for in Chicago is killing a woman. Our juries may be yellow, but, by God, they're sentimental! I'll guarantee your safety.'

'Are you God?' she asked scornfully.

'Not in Cicero,' he said.

She mocked him.

'Dear friend! I am not afraid of Cicero, or the big house, or the little house. I shall never go there, never, never! I love myself too much for that.'

'You don't know Tony Perelli,' said Kelly, but she smiled at this.

'What does it matter?' she asked. 'You try to make me so mad, and I don't want to be mad with anybody. I want to go away with a lovely feeling towards everybody.'

This was news to him.

'You're going away, eh?' he asked eagerly.

She nodded.

'Does Tony know?'—and when she shook her head: 'I wish I could do something for you.'

She laughed again.

'What can a great chief of detectives do?'

'Nothing,' he agreed. 'Just nothing. Not even for a right girl like you.'

'Do you think I am a right girl?' she bantered.

Forgetful for the moment of his real errand, he picked up his hat to go.

'I've done one nice thing for you—I haven't asked you who you're going away with.'

'And it would have been a waste of time if you had,' she said.

She looked past him. Tony was in the doorway, smiling at her. He was not like the Tony he had been earlier in the evening, but the Tony of old: considerate, tender.

'Ah, Minn Lee is entertaining you, Chief,' he said. 'You want to see me?'

He took the embroidery frame from the girl's hand.

135

'What is my pretty doing? That old Chinese dragon—he never gets any bigger. Look.' He displayed the frame to Kelly with a flourish. 'Such beautiful work, such delicate little fingers.' He kissed them. 'Now run away, little Chinese sweetheart—I'll see you presently.'

Kelly held out his hand.

'Good-bye, Minn Lee.'

She hesitated for a moment, then took it and dropped a little curtsy.

Tony was interested.

'Eh? That's the first time I see you shake hands, Mr. Kelly.'

'It's the first time I've met anybody in your apartment that I've wanted to shake hands with,' said Kelly shortly.

He looked at the door through which Minn Lee had passed and closed it.

'You're poison all right, Perelli. I've often wondered what you are and now I know. Have you any Jewish blood in you—no? Maybe Judas was a half-bred Sicilian. Sit down.'

For a moment murder glowed in Perelli's eyes, and then he turned with a mechanical smile to the watchful Angelo.

'Sit down in my own apartment? Angelo, you heard?'

There was no response from his cautious servitor. Angelo was sensitive to a changed relationship between policeman and gangster. Kelly was talking like a man who knew something.

'My apartment in police headquarters is not so comfortable. The last eight gangsters who've sat down in my office chair are dead.'

Tony Perelli smiled again politely.

'They should have stood up as you do,' he said.

He turned again for support to his retainer.

'Mr. Kelly has a bad view of us, Angelo. If anything is wrong—find Tony Perelli. If the Mayor makes a bum speech—go find Tony. Vinsetti disappears—ah, search the apartment of poor Mr. Perelli!'

Angelo, in common decency, offered his agreement.

'I guess that's true, Chief.'

How like Perelli to bring up Vinsetti as an argument! The audacity of the move took Kelly's breath away.

'Vinsetti—h'm! He drew three hundred thousand dollars from his bank, he came here and was never seen again.'

Tony grinned. He had won in that game against police and squealer—won handsomely and was entitled to his triumph.

'Yes—and you had trailed him all day. He was with you all morning at Headquarters, squawking about his frien's —the great, big, hund'ed per cent squealer!'

'He came to this apartment,' insisted Kelly.

'An' I kicked him out,' Tony nodded. 'I don't want trouble with those kind of yeller guys.'

He was rather wishing now that he had not raised the matter and would have gladly changed the subject.

'He came to this apartment—and never left alive,' Kelly said.

Perelli looked round again and his lieutenant did what was expected of him.

'Say, Chief, that's all wrong; you was here ten minutes after.'

'Was there blood on the floor?' asked Tony angrily. 'Was there a body? Did anybody hear shooting?'

He was talking too much, had lost the grip he had had. A flippant challenge had been taken too seriously.

'Nobody would hear that,' said Kelly. 'I know all about that pistol of yours—grand for close-quarter work.'

Perelli burst into a fit of laughter which was only half simulated.

'He won't be reasonable! I kill everybody—Tony Perelli, Tony Perelli! If it wasn't for me there would be no newspapers—and if there was no Tony Perelli they would invent one!'

'Say, you oughter know better, Chief'—Angelo was pained—'than believe newspapers!'

'There oughtn't to be none,' said Tony venomously.

Kelly could understand his viewpoint.

'If there were no newspapers in Chicago there would be no police force,' he said.

Angelo wrinkled his nose.

'Then I say "To hell with the newspapers!"' was his comment, as he went out at a signal from his chief.

137

10

Tony Perelli was waiting. Something had happened: he was sensitive to a tense atmosphere. Kelly was playing with him; he had a disclosure to make—what was it to be?

There was one revelation to come, but it was early for Kelly to have had any news about Con O'Hara. Yet, exploring all reasons and possibilities, he could find no other explanation.

'Have you heard anything?' asked Kelly carelessly, as he took a long, black cigar from his waistcoat pocket, examined it critically before he bit off the end, and lit it with a leisure which was significant to the watching Sicilian.

Tony smiled.

'No, everything is quiet on the Western front,' he said.

'Fine!' Kelly's jaw set like a trap. When he said 'Fine' he did not mean 'Fine'.

He had news to give: Tony knew that. What was it? He was being played with cat and mouse fashion, and he resented the experience.

'Is that why you came,' he asked, 'to ask me for news? You can buy the *Tribune* for three cents. Why, Chief, I never thought you'd expect me to tell you what was happening in Chicago!'

Kelly walked up and down the apartment, his hands in his pockets, puffing slowly and enjoyably at his cigar. He surveyed the beautifully painted frescoes, the ceiling with its geometrical patterns enriched with replicas of Raphael, Tintoretto and the masters of the Italian school, and found them edifying. Then he turned slowly and faced the owner of this splendour, his steely eyes fixed upon him.

'Perelli, what are you making out of all your rackets?' he asked. 'A pretty big sum, I guess?'

Tony shrugged his shoulders.

'Well, I'll tell you because I am your frien',' he said with a hint of sarcasm. 'An' frien's should have no secrets from each other—is that right? I make a million and a half—two millions—a year. The expenses are heavy. A million I spent last year, mostly on the police. It's terrible how the police take bribes! Most of them are on my payroll. It is demoralising!'

Kelly smiled grimly.

'How much have *I* taken?' he asked, and Tony chuckled at the question.

He was bold to say what he had always thought, for he had no respect for a policeman who refused bribes, even as he despised those who accepted them.

'You, if you permit me, are a fool!' he said. 'We have a short time to live—it should be merry. It cannot be merry if we are poor. I haven't seen a ten-dollar bill for five years That is the way to live—not knowing that there is such small change as ten dollars.'

His gesture was a flourish. What he said he meant. For the moment he was impressed by his imperial magnificence, was carried away on the realisation of his achievements.

Kelly nodded.

'Your girls at Cicero know all about ten dollars,' he said significantly, and Tony Perelli was pained.

He was curiously touchy about this source of revenue at Cicero, and never failed to register an indignant protest and denial whenever such protest seemed called for. To those who were immediately associated with him in this business there was never any question about his interest in the Cicero houses. He discussed them as he would any other commercial enterprise, kept a very sharp watch on the financal operations of his evil trade, and generally took a pride in its prosperity. But let any reformer or uplifter, any preacher, dare associate the name of Perelli with these houses, and he rose, shrieking threats. He had once begun a suit against a Chicago newspaper, but was sufficiently intelligent to withdraw before the case came into court.

'My dear friend!' he almost wailed. 'My girls at Cicero! I have no girls at Cicero or at any other place. Those dreadful houses are not mine. I am incapable of taking such money—I thought you knew me better than that, Mr. Kelly.'

He was hurt, visibly so.

'I've never put a dollar into vice. Everybody who knows me will tell you that. My enemies say these things about me, but there is no proof—you know there is no proof!'

Kelly was sceptical.

'You have nothing to do with them at all? The Lion Inn, for example?' he suggested.

Tony smiled sadly.

'The Lion Inn! I know the place; it has been pointed out to me. Myself, I think there are lies told about it, but that is not my business. The house is not mine; I do not even know the guy who runs it.'

'Good!' said Kelly heartily. 'I'm glad to hear it. That was why I came.' He took a long pull at his cigar and sent a spiral of smoke up to the painted ceiling. 'The Vigilants raided the Lion Inn tonight,' he said; 'they turned the girls into the street and burnt the place to the ground.'

He saw the colour come and go in Tony Perelli's face. He might control his movements, but he could not govern his blood flow.

'What!' He came to his feet, one hand was trembling slightly. 'It's a lie!' He was breathless with fury. 'I should have been told by somebody long ago. . . . The Lion Inn cost a hundred thousand dollars!'

Then, with a snarl of rage:

'Vigilants! By God! They want a couple of typewriters workin' round there! Vigilants!'

He came up to Kelly and almost shook his fist in his face.

'Is there no police in Cicero?' he screamed.

The commissioner smiled broadly.

'You ought to know—you say they're on your payroll. What's the worry? It's not your house; you haven't got a cent invested. It doesn't matter to you, does it?'

'Vigilants!' Tony's voice was tremulous. 'Is there no law, then?' He threw out his hands in despair. 'A hundred thousand dollars, and not insured for a cent!'

He was making no pretence now. There was a hundred thousand dollars involved and he was face to face with the grisly reality. The Lion Inn . . . He made a rough mental calculation. Nearly two hundred thousand dollars that place had cost him.

Kelly had launched his thunderbolt and was ready to go.

'I'm through,' he said, and then, as a thought struck him: 'I've got one good bit of news—no lives were lost! As you're a humanitarian I thought that would please you.'

Tony was cold now, master of himself; that ice-box mind of his was functioning. His sense of humour might be deficient, but his sense of logic was irresistible. As Kelly turned he caught him by the arm.

'Wait one moment, Mr. Kelly. Let us speak straight.'

He was still a little staccato and breathless.

'You're a swell feller—I hand it to you. When you give me the green I pass; when you snap the red I stop. I know where I am with you. But there is only one way of running my racket and that is the way I go, eh? If one man is bumped off, or two men are bumped off, what does it matter? Are they innocent? Are they citizens? Tell me! They are hoodlums, murderers, bombers, hold-up men, vice men, everything! What does it cost to hang them in the State of Illinois? Fifty t'ousand dollars! Fifty grand! Lawyers, jurymen, judges, new trial, new witnesses—eh? It goes on for years before the hangman says "Step on it!" Four hundred people have been bumped off by gangsters—if you like, I am a gangster—by us! We save the State six million dollars—six cartridges for sixty cents, eh? That's cheaper than fifty thousand dollars. Outside the State Legislature there should be a statue to gangsters. We are benefactors—if you like, vermin that prey on vermin. It is unanswerable!'

This wild torrent came almost without a pause. Kelly listened, secretly admired, was openly amused.

'Fine,' he said. 'I've heard that so often that I'm beginning to know it by heart. Is Jimmy McGrath somebody's vermin?'

Tony Perelli looked at him quickly. What did he know or suspect?

'He's a nize boy,' he said suavely. 'I'm very fond of Jimmy. If the boy was my own brother I couldn't be fonder,' he said.

141

Kelly was sceptical.

'Con O'Hara—is he a brother too?'

'A swell feller,' agreed Tony.

'Where are they—these two gentlemen?' asked Kelly.

Tony grew mysterious, looked round for possible eaves-droppers, and lowered his voice.

'They've gone out to see a couple of girls—don't tell Con's wife that,' he said.

'You and Mike Feeney are all buddies now, eh?'

A disconcerting man, Kelly; he switched from one sub-ject to another so quickly that it was almost impossible to follow. Perhaps it was his way of catching a guy—gang-land knew of this idiosyncrasy of his, and gave it that interpretation.

'Sure, Mike Feeney and us are good friends. We've had our little misunderstandings,' said Tony.

'Was Shaun O'Donnell one of them?' asked the other.

Tony's glittering hands outspread in a helpless gesture.

'I know nothing except that everything is fine now,' he said.

Kelly pursed his lips, his cold eyes still fixed upon the man he hated.

'What price are you paying for everything being fine?' he demanded, and Tony's bewilderment was a little too elaborate.

'Mr. Kelly, you talk sometimes like a piece of German music which I cannot read or play.'

And now Kelly came to the point.

'Is somebody going to be put on the spot?' he asked bluntly.

Tony stared at him.

'Good God, no! I wouldn't do that to a yellow dog! Put a man on the spot! Why, that's murder, Mr. Kelly! It's yeller. You believe me . . .'

'Sure.' Kelly twirled his hat in his hands. 'You bit of yellow dirt! That's my good night to you!'

He saw the door open. Minn Lee looked through the narrow space that stood immediately behind her master. Then the phone bell rang. Kelly pointed to the instrument.

'Answer it,' he ordered. 'I told them I'd be here.'

And now Perelli saw the girl behind him, and turned to vent his fury on her.

'Get out,' he said under his breath, 'do you hear? . . . Take a man to your room and lock the door!'

Kelly took a step to the table as the phone rang again.

'No, no, I'll do it.' Perelli grabbed the receiver with a clatter. 'Yes?' he snarled. And then, with a complete change of tone: 'Police Headquarters? Yes, the Chief is here,' he said, and handed the phone to Kelly.

It was odd at that moment, when danger was threatening, when the attitude of the police had become menacing, when they could come to him and taunt him with the loss of the Lion Inn, that his mind should be completely and solely obsessed with the delinquency of one whom he had already betrayed and would betray further.

'He kissed you on the mouth!' His voice trembled. 'I saw him when he left you . . .'

Was this manufactured rage of his a salve to conscience, a self-justification for the murder he had committed?

Kelly was speaking on the phone. Minn Lee listened. Well she knew what message was coming through.

'Oh! . . . When did this happen? Huh . . . the boy Mc-Grath? Dead, is he?'

Watching, Tony saw her stiffen, and into her round, soft face came the radiance of a great exaltation.

'. . . Corner of Michigan and Ninety-fourth? Ah! Anybody else killed? . . . Nobody, eh? Only McGrath? . . . You're sure? . . . O'Hara wasn't with him?'

There was a crash. The ivory paper-knife with which Tony Perelli was fiddling dropped from his hand on to a small fish bowl. O'Hara wasn't with him? He could not believe his ears.

'I've got a squad car downstairs—don't touch the body till I get there.'

Kelly jammed down the receiver and, as he flew out, flung over his shoulder:

'Report at nine o'clock tomorrow at Police Headquarters.'

There came the slam of the door. Tony Perelli, livid with rage, spun round on the girl.

'You heard? To me—Tony Perelli—as if I were a dog!'

She did not hear him. She was gazing fixedly at something that he could not see or imagine. Her lips parted.

'Jimmy! Oh, Jimmy!'

'He's in 'ell!' snarled the man.

'He was in heaven tonight,' she breathed.

'Your lover, eh?' he sneered.

Though he said the words, he did not believe them. It was inconceivable that Minn Lee . . . Before the thought was completed she gave him confirmation.

'I love you—I didn't love him. But I gave him everything he wanted—everything! Oh, God, I'm happy! I've done something! I haven't been a waste!'

He recoiled from her as though she were a leper.

'You've—done something?'

She nodded.

'He knew he was going to his death, and he was glad,' she whispered.

Tony's hand went up to his damp brow.

'He knew he was going? Who told him that?'

'I told him.'

There was no defiance in her tone. She was simply making a plain statement. 'And he was glad. After he loved me . . .'

'He loved you?' The words came in a horrified squeak. 'He loved you—my woman?'

'His woman,' she said.

He could not articulate. She was telling him that which was horribly incredible. Suddenly he leapt at her, gripped her by the throat, and:

'Where is Con O'Hara?' she gasped.

The question brought him back to his senses with a crash. Con O'Hara . . . he was not there; his body had not been found. If Jimmy knew, then Con knew . . . There was danger, real gang danger, from a man who was fearless and, in his dull way, shrewd—a man who added to hurt vanity the spur of jealousy. Con had escaped from the trap.

'I'm going to my room,' said Minn Lee.

He flung out his hands.

'Go to hell, you damn' Chink woman! Go to hell!'

And then, as a thought struck him:

'Kelly—did he speak to you?'

144

She nodded.

'And you spoke to him? You told him something?'

She backed against the organ, and his hands gripped her savagely by the shoulder.

'You told him something? Two faces! You have six! You locked the door, eh? And you told Kelly . . .'

His fingers closed round her throat and choked her denial.

'You're a liar, you small, dirty little beast!'

Perelli's face was swollen; in his eyes was the glittering devil that was the soul of him.

'You know a hell of a lot, don't you? You know a lot!'

She wrenched her throat free.

'I know you killed Vinsetti.'

'You know that, eh?'

'You talked in your sleep,' she said.

He swung her round to the table and threw her across; reached for the heavy bronze that lay there to his hand. In his fury he was demoniacal.

'Don't kill me. I'm not afraid, but Kelly said they hang you if you kill a woman in Chicago. He wanted me to tell and take the reward, but I told him . . . I loved you.'

And then Perelli became aware that there was a spectator. Angelo was in the room. He stood stiffly at the door, his hands resting lightly on his hips. How near was Tony Perelli to death at that moment when he raised the bronze and Angelo Verona's fingers closed over the heavy butt of his automatic!

'You told him that, did you?' asked Tony thickly.

He looked at her, then at Angelo.

'You're swell, Minn Lee. All right.' He dismissed her with a gesture.

'What's wrong?'

There was a metallic quality in Angelo's voice which Perelli noticed.

'Send those women away—the whole party. They can go down the north elevator.' He gave his orders rapidly. 'Is Tomasino up there? Yuh? Who else?' impatiently.

'Toni Romano, Jake French, Al Marlo . . .'

'Send them right away. They're to take machines and scorch the town—and get Con O'Hara.'

'But . . .'

'He turned yeller.' Tony would not be interrupted. 'He let the kid go by himself. They got Jimmy all right. No shooting round this block,' he warned. 'Do you get that? Put a man downstairs to watch for him and give me the signal. If he comes here, I'll fix him.'

'Say, Con wouldn't know he was being put on the spot?' protested the bewildered Angelo.

'You're a fool too, are you? Why isn't he back?'

That was reasonable, too. But then, Tony was generally reasonable, even in his fury.

'Do you want all the women to go?'

'Yes,' said Tony, and then remembered. 'No, Con O'Hara's woman stays here.'

'Do I go with the boys?' asked Angelo.

'No, you stay also. And keep two or three men. When you've got rid of them I want the couch here. Now go— get these people away. Tell the boys there's a grand for the man who gets him.'

Angelo went out quickly, and Tony Perelli made his preparations. He had had to deal with crises before. In the case of Vinsetti, though the end had been inevitable, the opportunity had come unexpectedly, and it had nearly been spoilt by Minn Lee's sudden and unauthorised appearance. She knew, then, all the time! Tony had suspected this, though he had never asked her. It was unfortunate that this particular secret was such a vital one.

Minn Lee was strong, had a code of her own. Nothing was more certain than that Kelly would go starving for news if he waited for Minn Lee to feed him. Jimmy was dead—so that other incident was finished and done with. Anyway, Minn Lee was going, and he was not at all sorry that she had cut out half the regret which might have attached to their parting.

He turned out the main lights, leaving only the standard lamp burning. He took a gun, threw open the chamber and examined the shells carefully before he snicked back the cylinder. Then he put the gun under his hat, which he laid on the organ seat.

When Angelo came back with the news that they were gone, there were certain other preparations to make. In

146

the meantime Maria must be disposed of. While he was thinking of her she arrived, not in the best of tempers.

'Everybody's going home—this is certainly a party!' she complained with some asperity.

'My dear, sweet angel, we are business people,' he said smoothly.

She eyed him with a certain amount of disfavour. There was a time for business and a time for pleasure and she was no mixer.

'Business people, are you? I'd like to meet a few drinking people,' she said. 'Why are they going home?'

'They are going home,' he said pointedly, 'but I want you to wait.'

'How long?'

He told her, and her red lips curled.

'Without Con? Nothin' else you'd like?' she asked politely. 'I mean, don't miss anything because you're too bashful to ask for it.'

'I want you to stay,' said Tony sharply.

He was in no mood for badinage. There was something in his voice which startled her, and she got up quickly from the couch where she had been sitting.

'Something's slipped—what is it?' she asked.

'Yes, something has happened—a terrible thing,' he said. 'Jimmy is killed—I loved that boy!'

'Jimmy killed!' She could hardly grasp the fact.

And then it came to her that if Jimmy was killed Con might not have gone scot free.

'McGrath?' she said quickly and gasped. 'But he went out with Con—they went together! What in hell do you mean by "terrible thing"? Did somebody jump him off?'

Tony hesitated.

'Yuh,' he said, 'some of Mike Feeney's gang.'

She felt her knees go weak beneath her. This was not the first gang killing that had come into her purview or that had affected her life. She had known men, and women too, from whom she had parted overnight, and who had been picked up in odd attitudes on the post road in the morning, dead, and worse than dead.

'What happened to Con?' She hardly recognised the sound of her own voice. 'What happened to him?' she demanded shrilly. 'Ain't you got a tongue?'

She tried to push past him, but he caught her by the waist and swung her round.

'Let me go, you dirty Wop!'

She struggled desperately to beat his face with her hands.

'It's all right, I tell you. Con got away,' he insisted urgently. 'Kelly was here and got it straight through from headquarters on the phone.'

'Where's Con? Let me go!'

But he was not letting go. The one person she must not meet at this moment was Con O'Hara. She might talk; women like that did talk. If she added fuel to the blaze, who knew what might happen?

'You want him back right now, do you?' he demanded savagely. 'You wasn't feeling that way an hour ago,' he said. 'He'll be out all night, I tell you—dodging the police. They think he killed Jimmy.'

The last was an invention on the spur of the moment, and he found some pride in it.

'I'm going home to wait for him,' she said.

'You've got your sleeping things—there's no need for you to go home. You'll stay here. If you go to your house you'll have the coppers at your place all night. . . . You will stay here.'

'Like hell I will!'

She fought at him, but was powerless. He had her face in his hands and forced it upwards to his; his lips closed over the red mouth. . . .

'Con will kill you,' she mumbled.

'Are you staying?'

She went limp in his arms.

'Till Con comes back,' she murmured.

Tony became his normal, polite self; opened the door for her.

'You know your room—I chose it for you. Con's over the Indiana line by now,' he said comfortingly. And then 'He'll not come back tonight.'

'Nothing'll happen to him?' she asked.

He shook his head.

'Not a damn' thing.'

'You're sure?'

He said he was very sure—too sure for his own peace of mind.

He went with her a little way along the passage, waited until her door closed. The click of the key made him smile. How very respectable were these unrespectable people!

Angelo was waiting, two of the dark-chinned men with him. By the time Tony had got back to the salon there had appeared a new article of furniture, a large, red couch and, spread before it, an extensive square of cloth of the same colour as the carpet. Vinsetti had seen that couch and had remarked upon it, partly because it was not quite new, and not as resplendent as any of the other articles of furniture in the apartment, and partly because he was a mental note-taker and could never resist the temptation to remark upon the obvious.

It was curious that Tony's mind should rest on Vinsetti at that moment. He mentioned the name to Angelo, who remained within the salon.

'You remember, eh? . . . That squealer?'

'Yuh.' Angelo was not concerned with past history, but with the history that was to be made. 'Romano will get him, anyway,' he said.

'You've fixed the alarm?'

Angelo glanced up at the little switch and nodded.

'She's O.K. But he won't come back. Who tipped him off?'

He was standing at the door, listening for the sound of the elevator.

'The kid,' said Tony surprisingly, and Angelo gaped at him.

'The kid? Why, he was bumped—he didn't know he was being put on the spot or he wouldn't have gone.'

Tony nodded.

'He knew.'

There was a sense of tension, of suppressed irritation. The very slightest sound brought the eyes of both men to the door.

'Knew he was being put on the spot and went to it?' said Angelo incredulously.

'Yes, yes, yes.' Tony was impatient. 'Don't ask me any more questions, Angelo. That is how it was—he knew he was being put on the spot and he went to it.'

'Is that so?' Angelo whistled. 'Would you believe that? But who told him—Jimmy—what was going to happen?'

'Minn Lee,' said Tony harshly. 'That's who told him. She took him to her room, Angelo.' His voice trembled. 'Took him to her room, you understand? . . . While we were all here she took him to her room and locked the door! By God, she shall know something about this!'

The thin smile of Angelo Verona was difficult to interpret.

'I guess she knows enough to keep her mind occupied . . .'

The buzzer sounded; it was the signal that Con O'Hara had been sighted outside. Angelo mopped his brow with a silk handkerchief.

'Gee, I didn't think he'd come back! They oughter get him in the hall.'

'This block belongs to me,' said Tony sharply. 'I want no scandal here. The man who gets him in the hall will be got—I've said it!'

Again the warning buzz. Con O'Hara was inside the building. A warning gesture from Perelli.

'Get out,' he whispered. 'If I miss him you get him. But I want everything quiet.'

The man sidled from the room, and Tony stood near the organ where his hat rested, and waited. He heard the front door open. Something rustled in the hall, and then the door of the salon moved slowly, opened, and a gun came in. It covered Tony Perelli where he stood, the arm extended. The space between door and post widened. Con O'Hara came sideways into the apartment. His hat was on the back of his head, and in his white face was death.

Tony had picked up his hat.

'Hello, Con!' he said in a conversational tone. 'You're back, are you? All the party's gone home. I'm going for a walk—come with me.'

He stepped fearlessly down until he stood in front of the big, red settee.

'One of us ain't going to walk far.'

Con O'Hara spoke like a man who had been running upstairs. He was in a white heat of fury. If there was anything which held him in check it was the crook's unfailing suspicion of the stories that are told to him by his kind.

But Jimmy must have spoken the truth, for he had died to prove it.

'One of us is going to stay right here,' he went on, 'and that one is you—you double-crossing Wop!'

Tony smiled.

'Are you drunk or somep'n'?' he asked. 'Did Jimmy give the copper my letter?'

Con O'Hara was breathing heavily through his nose. He had to take hold of himself to control his voice.

'Yeh!' He nodded slowly. 'And he's dead. . . . I watched it. . . . I didn't believe that crazy kid—that you were putting us on the spot. So I watched, and a car drove up and they poked a machine-gun on him. They waited a while—lookin' round for somebody else—me!'

Bewilderment and pain were the dominant expressions on Perelli's broad face.

'I don't understand—what do you mean, Con? You think I, Antonio Perelli, put you on the spot . . .'

'Yeh, that's what I mean,' said the other grimly.

'My bes' man?' said Tony, pained. 'And Jimmy, my bes' friend?'

'Where's my wife?'

'She's gone home,' said Tony, and flicked a speck of dust from his shoulder.

'Gone home, has she? She's here!'

Tony grinned.

'Ah, you're stupid! Be sensible, Con. If your wife was here, would I be going out?'

'You're not goin' out,' said O'Hara between his teeth. 'Gimme that hat!'

He stretched out his left hand and snatched the black felt hat from Tony Perelli's hand. As he did so the gun that was concealed by the hat spat once. It was not a loud report— the explosion was almost deadened, and outside the room you might not have heard it. Con's pistol dropped to the ground; he clasped his hands over his body. He turned slowly to fly; then his strength left him and he fell on his knees. Perelli fired once again, this time very truly, caught the swaying figure by the neck and flung him face forward on the outstretched cloth.

'Don't soil my carpet, you bastard!' he said.

151

11

Maria heard the sound of the organ playing and came back to the salon. The big couch had gone. She had not seen it, and so she did not miss it. It was a long time afterwards, when the police asked her about a couch, that she denied its presence. When she was shown the red sofa with the hollow seat, where a man could be hidden and moved, she could not identify it. She came back to see Perelli and hear him play—but not for long.

There are curious stories told about that night, but this much is certain: when she gave her lips to Perelli, all that was mortal of Con O'Hara was within a dozen yards of her.

It was a very uneasy woman that went home to discover whether her husband had returned in the night. She came back to Tony's apartment, more troubled than she ever remembered being.

Angelo Verona sat in his shirt sleeves at the big refectory table in the salon, and he was very busy, for this was pay day. Before him were three stacked heaps of currency, and he was sorting out ill-written accounts when she arrived.

She liked Angelo—but then, everybody liked Angelo. He was the nearest thing to a Big Shot in Chicago, would one day be controlling large and important interests, unless fate dealt unkindly with him, and a disgruntled friend of Mike Feeney's wrote 'finish' to a most interesting chapter of life.

He was on the telephone when she came in.

'. . . No, Mr. Perelli's not in. Who's that? . . . *Chicago Daily News*? Well, get to hell out of this! We ain't got nothin' to tell newspapers, we don't know nothin', see? He ain't in!'

He slammed down the receiver and became aware of her presence.

'I thought we'd lost you,' he said sarcastically.

'Was that Con?' she asked.

He sighed. She must have heard most of the conversation, and if she could confuse the *Chicago Daily News* with Con O'Hara ...

'On the wire? No, baby, that was not Con. Unless Con has gone and joined the staff of the *Chicago Daily News*— as crime investigator, maybe?'

She was oblivious of sarcasm, even sarcasm that did not err on the side of subtlety.

'He hasn't been back?'

'No,' said Angelo, addressing himself to his labours.

She shook her head and sighed.

'I've been sitting waiting in my home since nine o'clock —not a word from him.'

In truth she had been rather relieved to find that Con was not at home when she reached her apartments. But that relief had soon developed into a great uneasiness. She had not, however, sat down and twiddled her thumbs; rather had she spent her time in overhauling her wardrobe and making herself as attractive as the new adventure demanded.

'I guess he took the Limited,' said Angelo, without looking up. 'He was talking last night about going to Detroit. Say, why do all these guys go to Detroit ... ?'

'He didn't say anything to me about going to Detroit,' she said. 'Has he wired?'

'No,' said Angelo wearily, 'he didn't wire.' And then he remembered: 'They phoned up for you from Police Headquarters,' he said.

'For me?' She was aghast. 'What did they want? They don't know anything about me.'

'I guess not,' said Angelo. 'They only just asked if you were there, and I said "What a question!" They didn't ask any more.'

There was relief in her sigh.

'I wish I'd heard from Con.'

Angelo put down his pen. There was no sense in trying

to work with this human talking machine spitting out tri-
vialities.

'Say, why are you worrying, Mrs. O'Hara? In this racket
a guy has gotta jump around and be away for weeks. We
ain't sellin' chewing-gum.'

She was not comforted.

'No news in the papers?' she asked.

Angelo ran his fingers through his hair and surveyed her
balefully. There were many things he could say, but he
knew enough of what was happening to use discretion.

'No. The State Attorney's had his house bombed, but
who the hell cares about that? And there's a lot about
Jimmy.'

'I read that,' said Maria. She took a cigarette from a
jewelled case and lit it. 'Poor kid!' She offered this tribute
with sincerity.

'Yeh,' said Angelo. 'Very, very sad.'

And it was the fact that he meant what he said. He had
read every line about Jimmy. The senselessness of it! Jimmy
was a real feller; there was not the raw material of a
squealer in him. He could have been sent back home or to
the coast, or lifted out of the country, and he would never
raise the pencil of a squeak stenographer. Angelo had wondered why, and had supplied very shrewdly his own solution to the mystery.

'Jimmy and Con went out together,' she went on. 'Do
you remember that, Angelo?'

He nodded.

'There's something wrong.' She was uneasy, insistent.

The situation called for a more dramatic lie. Angelo
got up from his chair and came down to her.

'Now listen, Mrs. O'Hara. I'm going to tell you something. Con came back here in the middle of the night . . .'

This brought her to her feet in a fluttering agitation.

'What! You saw him?'

'Yeah,' said Angelo. 'I saw him, and it was very, very
awkward.'

'He came here,' she gasped. 'Did he ask where I was?'—
breathlessly. 'Had he been home?'

'Why, no.' Angelo could improvise an ordinary lie with
great glibness, but here were complications. 'I told him

you were sleeping with Minn Lee and that Tony was out looking for him.'

'He didn't want to come upstairs or anything?' she asked faintly.

Angelo smiled.

'I wouldn't have let him do that.'

She smiled. The quick rise and fall of her bosom told Angelo that Con had been no negligible quantity.

'That's mighty swell of you,' she said. 'I would have died!'

'Somebody would have died,' said Angelo drily, 'but you don't look a die-er to me.'

'On the level, Angelo'—she picked up the cigarette she had dropped, covering with her toe the little burn it had made on the carpet—'on the level, where has Con gone?'

'Where I said,' said Angelo sharply. 'Detroit. The bulls were after him for a racket that happened in New York. They saw him on the street and he just ducked in time.'

Here indeed was news. Maria considered it.

'Was it for Joe Lereski?'

'Joe who?'

'Lereski,' she repeated.

Angelo shook his head.

'Never heard of the man. He didn't tell me—some dame squealed on him.'

Maria's mouth opened wide.

'Gee, I'll bet that was his wife!'

'I didn't know he was married,' said Angelo cynically, but cynicism and sarcasm were alike wasted.

'That's what he tells me,' she said with a shrug, 'but you can't believe these men. He didn't leave any message for me?'

'Yeah.' Belatedly Angelo remembered certain instructions he had received that morning. 'He said you were to stay along here till you heard from him—with Minn Lee.'

She was still uncertain whether to accept or reject his story.

'Yes, but he had no money, Angelo.'

'I gave him two grand—and got hell from Tony for giving it,' he said.

He put his hand under her chin, and lifted her face.

155

'Did you have a marvellous time, baby?'

This brought her back to a sense of her position, or the position she was destined to occupy.

'Keep your paws to yourself, will you?' she said, as she struck his hand away. 'Where's Mr. Perelli?'

'We call him Tony round here,' beamed Angelo. 'He's at Police Headquarters—him and his lawyer. You'll like living here; it's the swellest apartment in Chicago.'

Maria looked at him suspiciously.

'Where did you get that expression—"living here"?'

'Tony gives grand parties,' Angelo went on. 'He claims he's goin' to Paris this year, too. Ever been to Paris?'

She shook her head.

'It's in France,' he volunteered, 'a swell place. It's where Napoleon was. Heard of him? I only heard about him myself the other day.'

'But he could have phoned from Detroit!' Maria was harping on the old key.

'He's been dead for years,' said Angelo, wilfully dense. And then: 'Oh, Con? Sure, he could phone. And I suppose there ain't any headquarters men down at Central tapping the wires? Good morning, Minn Lee.'

She looked radiant and fresh, a woman without a care in the world, this Minn Lee in her white frock with its green embroidery. She had a book and a long-bladed sheath knife in her hand, and stood at the big table, cutting the pages of a French novel. Maria was momentarily embarrassed.

'Why, Mrs. Perelli, I didn't see you this morning. I don't know what you'll think of me, sleeping here all alone without my husband.'

Minn Lee looked at her and seemed amused.

'I knew you were staying,' she said.

Here was the first check.

'It was awful about my husband not getting back.'

The smile left Minn Lee's face, and she shook her head. 'Poor girl!' she said.

'How's that?' said Maria, uncomfortable, and ready to be resentful.

'I said "poor girl",' smiled Minn Lee. 'I meant that. Tony didn't phone again, Angelo?'

He did not answer but, leaning over, took the knife from her hand and examined it.

'Say, Minn Lee, you oughtn't to use that knife,' he said. 'It's razor sharp.'

'Tony broke the paper-knife last night,' said Minn Lee, and took the knife back from him. She examined it and drew her little thumb along the edge. 'Do you think I shall kill somebody?'

Maria was not to be led from a subject in which, by the very nature of things, she figured most prominently.

'Ain't it awful not hearing from Mr. O'Hara? That man worries me sick.'

'Tony knows where he is,' said Minn Lee. 'Why didn't you ask him?'

Maria sat stiffly upright, her chin raised.

'I have not seen Mr. Perelli since he knocked on my door and said good night,' she said firmly. 'I didn't open the door either, because it was locked. I always lock my door in a strange house. I don't know what you're laughing at, Mrs. Perelli.'

'I wasn't laughing—if I was, I'm sorry. I'm rather happy today—are you?'

Angelo, an interested audience, looked sharply at Minn Lee, but there was no evidence of malice in her eyes or in her tone. Sensitive though she was to criticism, direct or oblique, Maria saw no challenge in the question.

'Happy? My God! Haven't you got a heart—with that poor kid all shot up in the morgue? I suppose it's being Chinese that makes you so hard?'

Minn Lee laughed softly.

'Yes, it's the Oriental in me,' she said.

She took up her book and walked out on to the balcony. Maria waited until she was out of earshot.

'What's that—"Oriental"?' she asked, in a low voice.

'I guess it's the Chinese word for Chinese,' said Angelo, and Maria nodded.

'I'll remember that—Oriental! I'm always willing to learn. A very nice lady, Mrs. Perelli.'

'Tony won't ever find a better one,' said Angelo.

It was the wrong comment to offer, and he knew this.

'I wouldn't say that,' she said, a little nettled.

'Of course you wouldn't. I didn't expect miracles,' said Angelo.

She put up her hand to stifle a yawn, and came lounging up to the table, turning over the money and reading the accounts, an action that irritated Angelo unreasonably.

'What are you doing? Are you Mr. Perelli's clerk? Look at that money—my, what a lot!'

'The root of all evil,' said Angelo, tidying the scattered heap. 'Gee, the guy that said that didn't know anything!'

Minn Lee had come back from the balcony and had set down her book on the couch. Angelo noticed apprehensively that the knife marked her page.

'Oh, yeh! I forgot to tell you, Mrs. O'Hara, that Tony's the grandest feller in the world about money.'

'And he's got two hundred silk shirts,' mocked Minn Lee.

'You don't say!' Maria was impressed. 'I like a man to be dressy. Con's mighty particular about his clothes.'

Angelo thought he would get over all that.

The front door slammed. Nobody slammed the door of the apartment but Tony. He came in, tore off his scarf and his hat and flung them at the waiting servant.

'Why, Mr. Perelli!' said Maria loudly. 'I haven't seen you since last night.'

He did not heed her. He walked quickly to the balcony and looked over. Then coming back, he fell into a chair.

'Are you tired?' asked Minn Lee.

'I've had a 'ell of a day,' he groaned. 'I was at Police Headquarters since nine till an hour ago.'

'Chief Kelly did the entertaining?' suggested Angelo, and Tony's face twisted with fury.

'I'll tell you how that pig entertained me! Get Supreme Court Judge Raminski on the wire. I'm going to make that damn' cop eat off my hand!'

'Supreme Court Judge Raminski!' gasped Maria, and well she might be astonished, for Judge Raminski was the Great White Chief of Chicago politics, a man holding a high judicial position and, more important, one of the real bosses of Chicago.

'I'm all in,' said Tony. 'They drove me here and there till I was dizzy. From Police Headquarters to the City Hall, from the City Hall to Police Headquarters, from Police Headquarters to the morgue, then to the place where poor little Jimmy was found.'

'Your call is through.'

Angelo handed the receiver to his chief, and Tony instantly came to energetic life.

'Is that Supreme Court Judge Raminski? . . . This is Perelli speaking—Antonio Perelli.' And then, fiercely: 'Say, what the hell do you mean by letting Kelly push me all over the place? You're supposed to have a pull, ain't you, eh? . . . I swung two wards for you at the election, didn't I? . . . Maybe I didn't give you fifty grand for the election fund? Eh? . . . I know, I know—you'll talk to Kelly—you'll talk to him! You're supposed to be the big noise at the City 'All; you're a grand feller, you'll be a senator some day, you will! . . . Yes, yes, you will, by God! You get Kelly fired—that's what you do!'

He threw back the receiver.

'I'll fix that guy!'

To a judge! Maria had never realised the greatness of her captor till that moment. To talk to a judge . . . a man who sentenced people for life.

'Say, talking to a judge like that . . .' she began.

'You ought to hear him talk to the President!' said Angelo, and Tony snarled round at him.

'Don't be smart, Angelo. Get me a drink—Chianti—anything . . .'

But Minn Lee was already running from the room on this errand.

'Did you go to Cicero?'

Angelo nodded.

'Yeh. They didn't do nothing to the Lion Inn—it's just slag and smoke.'

'Wait a minute.' Maria had a passion to be in all conversation. 'I read that. It was a vice house, wasn't it? I'm damn' glad! I wish the Vigilants would burn 'em all! Men who live on that kind of racket are just dirt!'

Tony restrained himself with difficulty.

'Oh, indeed? You don't know anything about it.' His voice rose almost to a shout. 'A hundred thousand dollars

'. . . just because a lot of bums are trying to suppress human nature.'

'Human boloney!' scoffed Maria. 'It ain't human nature to treat women as if they was cattle, just to put a little more jack into a yeller dog's bank roll! They oughter give 'em the rope for it!'

Angelo was making signals which his employer could not see.

'Oh yes,' said Perelli, his voice tremulous with anger. 'Because you are all hypocrites and will not see that human bein's are human bein's, because you will not see with the eyes of truth—that these girls are perhaps savin' innocent girls from ruin.'

'It doesn't save many of 'em, believe me,' said Maria.

'Ah, you know all about it, eh?'

'Sure, she knows all about it,' said Angelo. 'She's right, Tony.'

This time Tony caught his signal and with an effort he laughed.

'I suppose so,' he said. 'But I'm thinking of the poor girls —they've lost everything.'

Minn Lee came back with the wine at this moment and Maria turned to her.

'Gee, that must be an awful life, eh, Mrs. Perelli?'

'I didn't hear,' said Minn Lee.

'These houses at Cicero . . .'

'Will you be quiet?' said Tony angrily. 'How can you get inside their minds and tell whether it's awful or nize? It may be swell for them.' He looked at Minn Lee with an encouraging smile. 'A girl in charge of a house is like a princess, with a fine suite and grand furniture. She meets the friends she wants . . .'

He suddenly took Minn Lee's hand in his.

'You are all silly,' he said. 'Well, my darling, I didn't see you last night. I was so worried about poor Jimmy that I slept in my study.'

'Study . . .' began Maria.

'Yeh; it's the place where he sleeps,' said Angelo, as he carried his money basket out of the room.

'Did you see Jimmy?' Minn Lee asked, in a voice so low that Maria could not hear her.

160

For once his nerve failed him and he could not look her in the eyes.

'Yes,' he said; 'he looked wonderful. He was smiling as if he was having a good joke.'

She saw his face twitch. That good joke of Jimmy's had made an impression upon him.

'I expect he is,' said Minn Lee. 'You heard nothing more —I mean, of how he died?'

Tony shook his head.

'No, he was just alive for one, two, three seconds when the patrolmen got to him.'

'Poor kid,' said Maria conventionally.

'Why "poor kid"?'

Minn Lee stopped on her way from the room to look down at her. There was a strange smile in her eyes, a serenity which impressed the woman so that she did not speak until the door had closed on the white-dressed little figure.

'She gets me guessing, that woman,' said Maria irritably.

She got Tony guessing too, and wondering. And his chief and most troublesome wonder was how life might be without Minn Lee. Could he endure that she should go away from him as the others had gone, and pass to the vicarious possession of the moneyed patrons of the big house? He had flashes of horror at the thought. There were moments when the idea was unendurable, revolting. It was his boast, however, that he was a business man, and he had never hesitated to sacrifice life and human happiness to the full accomplishment of his designs.

She got Maria guessing; but Minn Lee got him guessing about himself. It had seemed so easy when he had made the plan, and she had played into his hands so perfectly, given him all the excuse he wanted, if indeed he wanted any. He did not really know Minn Lee; she had a wall around her mind, and he had never found the door.

He looked at the lovely woman who was to supplant her. There was no wall around Maria's mind. He sank down by her side and put his arm about her.

'My beautiful girl, you have missed me all day?'

She looked sideways at him—a sly and intimate glance of understanding.

'Do you still love me?'

He pressed her tightly to him, and found her evasive lips. . . . She pushed him away from her and came to her feet with a frown.

'Tony, honest, I don't want that stuff now. . . . I'm all nerves, as jumpy as a cat. Where's Con?'

His surprise at the question was slightly exaggerated.

'Con?' he asked. 'Didn't Angelo tell you?'

There was suspicion in the glance she shot at him.

'Yes, he told me, but you didn't. It seems to me you birds spend your time thinking up lies to tell me. Why should Angelo know . . .'

'Angelo did know,' interrupted Tony, 'but that feller keeps everything under his hat.'

She searched his face.

'On the square, is it true what he said about Con going to Detroit?'

Tony crossed his heart with a great gesture, and the smile became a laugh.

'Do you know what I thought? That you'd sent him away —you're so damned clever. I thought you had some scheme for getting rid of him last night. You've certainly got brains.'

Tony smiled complacently.

'Maybe,' he said.

One matter had to be settled. Maria was, by her own code, a square dealer, and she took a practical view of life. Partnerships in her strange world were dissolved and re-established without the formalities of Reno. They ended and began abruptly; there was no drift, no interregnums of indifference. When a feller was through he was through; when a girl quit she just quit; and that was all there was to it. And she had quit, so far as Con O'Hara was concerned.

'Now, listen,' she said. 'When he comes back I'm going to tell him everything.'

'Con? That's O.K. by me,' said Tony.

She expounded her philosophy.

'I don't believe in deceiving a man—I mean, when the other gentleman doesn't mind—it's mean.'

Perelli smiled broadly.

'That's a beautiful thought,' he said.

'Yes, I have them sometimes,' admitted Maria, and then became more serious. 'He'll raise hell. Con's a pretty tough guy,' she added warningly.

Tony nodded.

'Everything like that he told me,' he said.

'I was through with him, anyway,' said Maria. 'You can't respect a guy who ain't got the money to treat you right.'

There was another and a more delicate matter to be discussed. By Maria's code certain vital adjustments had to be made. She jerked her head in the direction of the door.

'What will you do with . . . ?' She did not mention Minn Lee by name. 'That's got to be fixed, Tony.'

It had to be fixed, indeed, and it was not so simple as he had thought. He shrugged his shoulders.

'I'm through too,' he said. 'She doesn't love me any more, and'—he lowered his voice—'she went wrong!'

Maria was frankly shocked.

'It just goes to show that you can't trust these Ornamentals . . .'

The name produced no reaction. She coughed embarrassedly.

'. . . these foreigners. But you're not going to leave her flat, Tony? I'm strong for women being treated right. When I took on O'Hara I made him stake the girl he was running around with—yes, sir!'

Tony stroked her head tenderly.

'That's nize! That's what I like to hear you say. Nize girl, Maria. There ain't many like you who'd think that way.'

'That's my weakness,' said the woman, 'playing square.'

She went on to tell him other things about herself, mostly of a complimentary character, but he was not listening. He had remembered Kelly's promise, which was almost a threat.

'I'm coming up to see that new woman of yours,' had said Kelly with brutal directness, and displaying a disconcerting knowledge of Tony Perelli's private life. Now he passed the information to Maria, and she was disturbed.

'What does he want with me? I don't know a thing about your racket,' she said, in alarm.

163

Tony patted her hand.

'It's noth'n', honey. Maybe he wants to talk to you about Jimmy—you met him.'

Maria had certainly met the boy, but hardly remembered him.

'Or perhaps he will talk about Con,' said Tony carelessly. 'But, anyway, let him do the talking.'

She smiled contemptuously.

'Why, if he thinks he can make a fool out of me . . .'

'And don't get mad at him. That's his speciality, making people mad,' warned Tony. 'Oh, God, how he makes you mad! And if you get mad you talk.'

She had all the confidence of her kind.

'He'll be in a jam before I'm through with him . . .' she began, but he stopped her.

'Don't get Con O'Hara's complex, for the love of Mike! Don't think that you're so clever that all you've got to do is to hand him a few wisecracks to get away with it.'

She was now thoroughly alarmed. She had nothing to get away with. She said so.

Angelo stood in the doorway and beckoned him. He thought it was Kelly, but it was quite another type of visitor that his lieutenant had to announce.

'Mike Feeney is outside. Will you see him?'

Tony looked at him incredulously.

'Mike Feeney—where?'

Angelo jerked his thumb over his shoulder.

'Has he brought his gang?'

A faint smile hovered at the corners of the young Italian's lips.

'No, I guess he left them outside.'

Tony gasped. Shaun O'Donnell wouldn't have let him do that. Shaun had brains—not much, but some.

'Why do you think he's come here?'

Tony remembered a certain important matter he had to discuss with Angelo. In truth he had never forgotten it, but it had been kept in the background of his mind. Here was an opportunity. He made an excuse and sent the woman into the little salon. Then he came back to the younger man.

'Angelo,' he said simply. 'I've been talking to the lawyers,

164

and the accountant was there. And I met a guy who said you'd sent away a million dollars to Europe.'

Angelo nodded gravely. It was a grave matter. The money was his, but it might not be transferred to the security of a European bank without a possibility of the most unhappy consequences. The transfer had been carried out with great skill and secrecy; the operation had covered six months of time. But gangland has its spies. Neither the lawyer nor the accountant would have told Tony Perelli. He must have had it by some bank clerk—but that was a matter of indifference.

'Sure,' said Angelo. 'I have an old mother and a sister in Italy, and I'm settin' 'em up.'

'You've got a cabin in one of the Canadian ships, they tell me, Angelo?'

Tony's voice was as silken as ever, but it lacked one imponderable quality. Angelo knew that he was guessing.

'That's a lie,' he said instantly.

Anyway, it was impossible that Tony or his informers could have discovered the hiring of a cabin. It had been carried out through a London agency and a London bank.

Tony Perelli thought this over, squeezing his lower lip and studying the pattern of the carpet. Then abruptly he changed the subject, which was a bad sign.

'Cover all ways out in case of accident,' he said. 'I've got to settle with Feeney sooner or later. Did you fix he got Bellini's for his birthday party?'

'Yeah. He fell for the menu. There was Irish stew on it.'

Again that long contemplation of the polished toes of his shoes, and then:

'Grand. Bring him in,' he said.

When he was alone he took an automatic from a drawer, slipped it in the holster under his armpit, and when Mike Feeney came in he was pacing up and down, his hands behind him, apparently lost in thought. He raised his eyes to greet his visitor.

'How are you, Mike?'

Feeney looked round the apartment with the greatest caution.

'Fine,' he said.

They eyed each other suspiciously.

'Get the book,' said Tony solemnly.

Angelo opened another drawer and produced a big ornamental Bible, which he laid on the table and opened in the centre. Tony took from each hip a long-barrelled revolver and laid them on the open page.

'There's mine,' he said.

Feeney hesitated, pulled a gun from his pocket, put it on the book, then suddenly snatched it up again, remembering certain earlier treacheries in his dealings with the Latin races.

'Hi, wait a minute,' he said. 'Is this Bible Eyetalian or Irish?'

'It is a hundred per cent American,' said Tony solemnly.

Feeney looked at the incomprehensible pages.

'Last time I done this I didn't get a square deal,' he said. 'The crook who provided it left out the Ten Command-ments.'

'They're all there, Mike,' said Perelli loudly; 'I paid a hundred dollars for that book at Letheby and Gothenstein's.'

Mike Feeney was satisfied. He knew Letheby and Gothenstein's: he got his shirts there, and they were square dealers.

He waited until Angelo was dismissed. He had never forgotten Shaun O'Donell's warning: 'Keep your eye on Tony Perelli, but two eyes on Angelo Verona.'

Feeney backed up against the wall, where he commanded a view of the door.

'Been to headquarters, haven't you, Tony?'

He was looking at the door, not at the man to whom he was speaking.

'Yeh—putting up a squeak on the high price of alcohol,' said Tony humorously.

Mike edged from the salon to the large folding doors that led to the Winter Garden, opened them slightly and peeped through. Tony watched him with growing annoyance. When he approached the second door:

'Somebody in there?' he asked.

'Yeah—a woman,' said Tony.

'Mind if I look?'

'Sure I don't mind,' said Perelli sarcastically. 'If you

haven't seen a woman I'll show you a picture of one. It's terrible to be so suspicious.'

Feeney looked and closed the door gently.

'I'm throwing a birthday party next week and I'd like to be there,' he said.

'Many 'appy returns,' said the other politely.

'Thanks—but I don't want no presents from you.'

Tony showed his teeth; this time he was really amused.

He knew why Feeney had come, and after a while he put his errand into words.

'Tony, you ducked one last night,' he said.

Perelli shook his head.

'Yes, you did.'

'Not on your life—Con O'Hara did all the ducking.'

Feeney's boys were sore about it. His host had the impression that he had come unwillingly, and that the visit had been forced upon him by the virulent incitation of his sister.

'They say you tipped off Con O'Hara.'

'Wouldn't they say that!' scoffed Tony. 'Why should I put him on the spot and tip him off, eh?'

Mike was still rolling his head from side to side, looking for some hidden danger.

'There's nobody there, Mike, on the level.'

Feeney's face twisted in a lop-sided smile.

'Yeah? Vinsetti did a quick slide out o' here, and he was a bigger shot than me. He came here and nobody saw him again . . .'

'That story's a reprint—forget it,' said Perelli. 'What are you frightened of, Mike? I ain't even got a rod.'

Feeney exposed his huge hands in a gesture.

'That's the same with me. I say, you either trust a guy or you don't trust him.'

He pulled up a chair and sat down, knee to knee with his gangster rival.

'I wouldn't be troublin' you, Tony, but there's me sister. She's just raising smoke. No woman likes to see her husband bumped off, especially if she's got sex appeal for him and she ain't got it for nobody else.'

'That is certainly unfortunate,' murmured Tony.

'She's not a good-looker, Tony,' Feeney was as confi-

dential as he was disparaging. 'In fact, she looks like hell
—I'm her brother and I know. And that makes it harder
for a dame to get over losin' her regular feller.'

He drew a long, quick breath and came to business.

'Now what about Con O'Hara? Come clean, boy.'

Tony Perelli did not answer at once. He looked thoughtfully at the dull-eyed clod before him, and wondered what
peculiar combination of circumstances had brought Feeney
to the leadership of a crowd of hoodlums who were anything but dumb.

'You needn't think about Con O'Hara,' he said at last.
'I took care of him.'

A light dawned on Feeney.

'So?'

'That's all,' said Perelli. 'I don't allow no guys to do me
dirt.'

'You took him for a ride . . .'

'Listen, Mike. Do I ask you your business? Do I ask
you what you do and how it is done? Do you and me go
shootin' our mouths all over Chicago?'

Mike raised his hand.

'I don't want to hear no more, Tony,' he said handsomely. 'I always knew you was a square guy and nothing
else but.'

A little buzzer sounded, and in a fraction of a second
Feeney was on his feet, a gun in his hand. Where it came
from, how it got there, Tony could not see, but the very
action half explained Mike Feeney's position as a gang
leader.

'What's the hell's that?' he asked. 'Stick 'em up!'

Tony was visibly pained.

'Why, Mike, you said you hadn't got a gun!'

'What was that buzzer?'

Tony heaved a deep sigh.

'It was Mr. Kelly. The janitor sent me a signal. That's
all.'

'Why is Kelly coming here?' demanded Feeney.

Tony groaned.

'To see Mrs. O'Hara. Why is Mrs. O'Hara here? Because she's my woman. Why is she my woman? Mind
your own damned business!'

Feeney put the gun into his pocket.

'I'm sorry . . .' he began.

'You don't trust me, Mike: that's what hurts me!' There was sorrow in Tony Perelli's voice. 'You said you hadn't got a rod, and you've got a rod!'

Again the buzzer sounded.

'I don't want to see Kelly,' said Mike Feeney.

'Do you suppose he don't know you're here? Go into the salon. Mrs. O'Hara is the lady in there. Don't flirt.'

He opened the door of the little salon.

'Mike, you'll never know how you've hurt my feelings,' he said, and Mike Feeney went, abashed, to the woman whose husband's death he had encompassed.

12

Chief of Detectives Kelly did not ordinarily lose his temper. He had to deal with a situation which was more complicated than any police situation in the world. Opposed to him was the most perfectly organised gang of law-breakers that had existed for three hundred years. They were men whose enormous wealth helped them to buy immunity from the operation of the law. Their friends were to be found in the most exclusive circles. They financed politicians and called tunes which were pleasant only to their ears.

In addition, they had the tacit approval of every citizen who secretly bought liquor. For these gunmen were no more than the escort which ensured the safe delivery of the booze which respectable citizens purchased, either for themselves or for the entertainment of their friends. And behind him Kelly had—what? A police force containing a large and corrupt patch; men who were in the pay of the liquor barons, high officers who accepted 'loans' from Perelli and his kind.

'The whole thing is hopeless—absolutely hopeless,' he said to his lieutenant before he left the office. 'Here's Raminski on the wire, telling me what I've got to do and how I'm to behave before his highness the Duke Perelli! And I've got to do it! I can either quit or go along administering the law, in so far as it can be administered without hurting the feelings of those gangsters who are friends of the men higher up! And I've decided,' he said grimly. 'I'm going! Some other guy can take on this job and break his heart over it—or gather in the golden corn. Perelli's won, so far as I'm concerned.'

The life of a police chief was a precarious one. His career

hung day by day upon a thread. A big gang murder, the discovery that one of his subordinates was running a crooked side game, the appointment of the inevitable committee of investigation—all or many of these things spelt ruin. A new chief would be appointed who would give optimistic interviews to the reporters; there would be energetic raids in all directions; speakeasies would be closed, gambling houses padlocked, slot machines confiscated; and the new broom, having worn itself down to the wood, would be out of action until a newer came to sweep.

Perelli . . . if he could only get Perelli! He had discussed the matter with Harrigan *ad nauseam*. But Perelli was almost cop-proof. He had his intelligence department, his band of trained lawyers, his hide-aways whither he could run in case of danger.

The chief was leaving headquarters when a clerk came running after him, and he went back to pencil down some very entertaining news. With a memorandum in his pocket he took the squad car and drove to Perelli's apartment for an interview which was destined to be their last.

Harrigan came with him, and to him Chief Kelly exposed the blank depression that was in his heart.

'Our only chance is if he loses Angelo,' he said. 'That's the wise kid of the bunch, Harrigan! Tony Perelli doesn't just know how much he leans on that bird.'

'The Feeney crowd will never catch him . . .' began Harrigan, and Mr. Kelly laughed harshly.

'It's not the Feeney crowd, it's the first law of nature that's beckoning Angelo Verona to the sunny south! That boy's wise! He'll be the wisest guy of all if he can take a powder on them without decorating the front page of the *Tribune* with a large cross to show the spot!'

They came to the block where Perelli's apartment was situate, and a man lounged up to the chief as he got out of the car.

'Mike Feeney's inside,' he said. 'There's his crowd of droppers on the other side of the street. And there's Perelli's crowd on this side, so I don't suppose that either gang will start something.'

Kelly left his lieutenant on the sidewalk and went up by the elevator to the big suite. Angelo admitted him, favour-

ing him with one of his sweetest smiles. He rather liked
Angelo, and grinned back at him.

As he lounged into the salon he saw the two chairs put
front to front and knew that a typical gangster conference
had been held. And there, too, was the open Bible, but
there was no sign of Feeney. He looked at the book, turned
a few pages, and bent his gaze upon the watchful Perelli.

'I haven't interrupted family prayers or anything, have
I?' he asked sardonically.

Tony smiled.

'No, we've just finished, Chief,' he said with elaborate
politeness.

Again Kelly's eyes roved around the room.

'I saw your little choirboys outside, and I've asked Mr.
Harrigan to pull in all in sight, in case they're contravening
the regulations by carrying guns.'

He closed the book slowly and stood with his back to
the table, watching Tony as he set the chairs in their places.
Angelo was looking unusually smart in a new cashmere
suit and a silk shirt of vivid pink.

'You're all spruced up, Angelo.'

Angelo looked at him and shook his head.

'I hate to see you happy, Chief: that's bad for somebody.'

The Chief chuckled.

'Is it, Angelo? Where's the beautiful lady?'

He did not particularise the beautiful lady, but both
men accepted the description as applying to Maria.

'She's in the small salon,' said Tony.

Kelly showed his teeth.

'Salon—Winter Garden—you guys certainly know how
to live—while you're living.' And then, with elaborate politeness: 'Would you be kind enough to ask Mrs. O'Hara
to see me?' he asked.

Tony was uncomfortable, and had reason to be.

'There's a friend of mine in with Mrs. O'Hara . . .' he
began to explain, but Kelly cut him short.

'I know—Mr. Michael Feeney. I'd love to meet him.'

'Do you want something from him?' asked Tony.

'Yeah,' said Kelly sardonically, 'his autograph! I'm col-
lecting 'em.'

He heard the deep sigh of Angelo and looked round.

'Gosh, I hate you cheerful!' said Angelo with feeling. 'I'd sooner you came and pushed everybody around.'

Mr. Kelly was amused.

'I'll push you around all right,' he called out to the retiring Angelo.

Then he laid his hat on the table, lit a cigar and regarded Tony Perelli with the greatest unfriendliness.

'We didn't tire you this morning, Mr. Perelli, or say anything to hurt your feelings or make you look undignified or anything?'

His extravagant concern increased the discomfort of Perelli. He had no sense of humour; sarcasm irritated and frightened him.

'I'd have had some flowers on the table,' Kelly went on, 'if I'd only thought of it. A few malmaisons or whatever is your favourite weed. I cannot remember at the moment what rare blooms you order for your funerals, but it would have been something expensive.'

'This is very amusing.' Tony's lip curled.

'So long as you're getting fun out of it,' said Kelly, 'that's all I ask. It seems I've got to be polite to you—Mr. Tony Perelli. That's what he calls you—"My friend Mr. Antonio Perelli".'

Tony's look of bland surprise might have deceived anybody but the one person he wished to deceive.

'My friend? I don't understand you. Who are you speaking about?'

'Supreme Court Judge Raminski came on the wire,' said Kelly. 'He thought we hadn't treated you right.'

Perelli shrugged his shoulders. He realised that perhaps he had been a little precipitate in lodging his complaint. Angelo had almost emphasised this point of view by his comment.

'We'll get some cushions for you the next time you come,' Kelly went on. 'The one thing I'd hate is to have Police Headquarters get a reputation for discourtesy.'

He looked round as Maria came defiantly into the room, followed by a sheepish Mike Feeney.

'Why, look who's here!' he said in mock surprise. 'Good afternoon, Mike.'

Feeney grinned uncomfortably.

'Good day, Mr. Kelly.'

'Don't say "mister" to me, Mike,' said Kelly, 'I'm just a copper who's due for a jolt. May I be permitted to ask why you're endangering your life in this'—he surveyed the room —'ecclesiastical brothel?'

'Tony and me's friends,' said Feeney.

The Chief was amused.

'Oh, that's why the flags are flying on Michigan Avenue!' Feeney looked at him enquiringly, edging towards the door.

'Do you want me, Chief?'

Kelly nodded.

'I want you like hell, but I can't get you, Mike.' He dropped his hand on the Irishman's shoulder. 'He'll get you.' He jerked his head towards Tony. 'And then you'll be no good to me—when you're in the mortuary. You've lost poor Shaun, eh?'

'Yeh,' said Feeney sadly.

'Too bad.' The sorrow in Kelly's voice was nicely simulated. 'Another martyr to science, eh? You bumped off one of the men who did it, and Tony bumped off the other.'

Maria spun round.

'How's that?' she said, but Tony's reassuring smile allayed for a moment her worst suspicions.

'Don't take any notice of the Chief: he's always pulling things like that,' he said. 'What do you want?'

Minn Lee, who had come softly into the salon, made no answer. She was looking at Kelly curiously.

'You got Jimmy McGrath and Tony got Con O'Hara, eh?' Kelly went on.

Maria bridled.

'That's a damned lie! Tony didn't go out all night.'

She tried to check the words, and could have bitten her tongue for her *faux pas*; but it was too late.

'You're in a position to certify that?'

'Yes, I am, Mr. Smarty,' said the girl defiantly. 'If you want to know where my husband is you'd better ask the New York bulls that chased him out of Chicago.'

Tony was looking at her hard, but for once the hypnotism of his eyes failed. And then the philosopher in him accepted the situation. After all, it had to be, this *dénouement*.

'The New York police chased him, eh?' said Kelly slowly. 'No detective from the New York Police Department is in this city. They wanted to pinch him for something he did in New York, is that it? For what? He wasn't wanted by the New York police. Who told you he was?'

Maria stood with averted face, a picture of dignity.

'That is all,' she said.

'Who fed you the yarn that he was running away from the police, and that that's why he disappeared?' asked Kelly and, when she did not answer: 'I know who told you —the man who bumped him off.'

She spun round at this, her face flaming.

'It's a damned lie—he's in Detroit.'

Kelly looked at her steadily for a moment and then came slowly towards her.

'He's in the Lake Side mortuary,' he said.

Her face went white and she dropped down to the couch.

'He was dropped on the beach some time in the night,' said Kelly. 'They found him ten minutes before I left my office.'

It was Angelo and Minn Lee who led the sobbing, hysterical woman from the room.

There was one interested spectator, to whom enlightenment came. Mike Feeney snapped his fingers.

'That's all square, eh?' said Kelly. 'All right, you can go.'

'Say, I know nothing about it, Chief,' protested Feeney.

'You wouldn't. You knew all about Jimmy McGrath, though,' said Kelly sternly.

'I never met the man,' wailed Fenney.

'Never met him, eh?' Kelly surveyed him. 'You're nearly a Big Shot now; you get somebody else to do your killing. Well, well, you were always an ambitious lad, Feeney. You were no sooner in the penitentiary for larceny than you aimed to get in for bank robbery.'

Feeney thought it expedient to change the conversation.

'Say, Chief, you wouldn't like to come to my birthday party? At the Bellini Restaurant. There'll be a swell crowd there—Judge Grichson, Judge Rosencrantz, Supreme Court Judge Aschen . . .'

175

'No, thank you,' said Kelly shortly; 'I don't study law I administer it.'

Feeney was calm before this rebuff, and waved a cheerful hand as he made for the corridor.

'Well, I'll say good-bye to you . . .'

'Mike!' Kelly called him back. 'I wouldn't have my birthday party in Bellini's if I were you.'

Tony and Angelo exchanged a swift glance.

'Eh?' said Feeney, staggered.

'That's all,' said Kelly. 'I shouldn't have my birthday party in Bellini's. Try some place up-town, then maybe you'll have another birthday.'

The dull Irishman looked from one to the other, and a glimmer of comprehension came to him.

'Thank you, Chief,' he said.

'Don't thank me.' Kelly showed his teeth in a mirthless smile. 'I want to see you croaked lawfully. Got a big interest in that restaurant, haven't you, Tony?'

Perelli did not answer, and Feeney drew a long breath.

'I may be dumb, but I ain't above learning,' he said, and went from the room.

'It's a waste of time asking you gentlemen about Con O'Hara,' said Kelly. 'I'll see the woman.'

'You can't see her, Mr. Kelly.' Minn Lee had arrived in time to hear the last words. 'She's like someone insane.'

'Like someone insane, and you left her?' roared Tony. 'Did you leave her there . . . just by herself . . . ? Get a nurse from the 'ospital—a doctor or somebody.'

He rushed from the room. They heard his 'I'm coming to you, Maria' float back through the closed door.

'That's the trouble with Tony Perelli,' said Kelly; 'he's got the heart of a child. I've often wondered that guy didn't run a children's home instead of running—the kind of places he's interested in.'

Minn Lee smiled wistfully.

'To you he can do nothing right, but to me he can do nothing wrong.'

Kelly shook his head.

'If there's one thing he doesn't deserve it's that. You're still here, I see?' And, when she nodded, 'I don't know whether I'm glad or sorry.'

Again that eerie little smile of hers.

'Be sorry today and glad tomorrow,' she said, cryptically.

Kelly walked to the door through which Tony had passed, opened it and looked out; then he closed the door softly and came back to the girl.

'When the patrolmen got up to Jimmy he was just going,' he said in a low voice; 'and he said two words—"Minn Lee".'

Her face was radiant.

'I thought I'd like to tell you that.'

As he turned to go she caught his hand and kissed it.

'Don't do that, kid,' he said gruffly.

'An old Chinese custom.' She was breathless and smiling. 'I am enlarging your knowledge of the East, Mr. Kelly.'

He patted the hand that rested in his and went out. She stood, transfixed, where he had left her, her hands lightly clasped, in her face a glory that no man had ever seen before. Then she came back to reality, picked up a cushion that lay on the floor and put it on the sofa and, walking to the balcony, took a long look at the spires and roofs of Chicago. She heard a confused jumble of sound; the door was flung open, and Tony came in, half carrying, half leading Maria O'Hara. He guided her to a chair and tenderly placed her in it, all the time murmuring incoherent and unintelligible endearments.

The dishevelled woman in the chair kept up an insistent babble of sobbing sound. Tony was oblivious of the little Chinese girl; his mind and thoughts were concentrated upon the woman for whose sorrow he was directly responsible.

'My poor, darling sweetheart . . .'

And then he saw Minn Lee.

'Get her some wine. Where's Angelo? Where's Kiki?'

She did not answer him, but went quickly from the room. Tony drew the girl's head to his chest.

'Oh, my dear, my dear!' He kissed her hair. 'So sorrowful and so lovely!'

'The hoodlums!' she said tearfully. 'To kill my Con!'

Tony's head went up.

'He shall have a swell funeral, Maria,' he said. 'I'll show Mike and his bums what a funeral is like. Twenty grand—

I don't care how much I spend, Maria.'

'You get the dirty dog who bumped him,' she snivelled. 'You do this for me, Tony—I'll give you every damned thing a girl can give . . .'

'Sure, sure,' said Tony, 'There won't be no Mike Feeney in the next phone book, believe me! I'll put the cross on that guy.'

Minn Lee brought the wine and Angelo, watchful, interested, came in her wake. Maria gulped down the liquor and made a face.

'It wasn't champagne,' she complained.

'You drink it,' said Tony, and then to his waiting lieutenant: 'Oh, Angelo, you fix poor Con. The swellest funeral ever. Spend money—roses, lilies, orchids, everything . . .'

Angelo looked up from the little book in which he was making notes.

'It would pay us to grow our own flowers,' he said, not without truth.

'And a silver casket,' said Tony, overcome by the magnificence of his own proposals. 'Get it from Philadelphia Better than Shaun's—much better.'

'He had angels on his,' suggested Angelo, his pencil poised.

'Get better.'

Angelo moved his head wearily.

'What the hell's better than angels?' he asked.

'Archangels,' snarled Tony. 'Do it at once.'

Maria had collapsed in his arms and he revived her. Presently they departed in an amazing medley of vehemence and denunciation. Angelo stood at the open door and watched them until they had disappeared into the room which was Maria's.

There was crisis here. Tony's attitude had changed a little—just a little, but sufficient for the keen-witted Italian to realise that the transition from Minn Lee to Maria would be accompanied by other transitions more violent and final.

He waited there for a long time, his hand on the edge of the door, looking down the corridor, thinking. There was a high-powered car within reach, a third elevator of which the police did not know, and a very fast motor-boat. Al

178

the avenues to safety—to life—were well greased.

Angelo had no illusions. He knew that, unless he took certain steps, he would that night rest under a tarpaulin, and all that would be left of him would be certain grisly photographs in the Records Department at Police Headquarters.

He came back with a sigh and closed the door gently.

'The way she's been missing Con since last night is something awful,' he said.

Minn Lee smiled faintly.

'Oh, you don't know; she may love him.'

Angelo shook his head.

'Loving men is foolish, Minn Lee, and she's everything but.' He chuckled as he took his seat on the settle of the organ. 'It's a grand life.'

'Where will you end, Angelo?'

'I was just wondering,' said Angelo drily. 'Until now I've never thought of it. There was all the chance I should be heading this gang one of these days—if somebody didn't bump me off. As it is'—his hands went out in an eloquent gesture.

He came down to her where she sat with her embroidery.

'Tony was saying there's likely to be some changes at Cicero. There's a new madam going in.'

'Is there? asked Minn Lee indifferently.

'I hope he won't choose somebody I know to take the place,' said Angelo carelessly.

'He'll find a woman,' said Minn Lee in a low voice.

'I surely hope he picks the right woman.'

Minn Lee shook her head.

'He won't pick me.' she said quietly.

'I surely hope he won't, for everybody's sake.'

She looked up in surprise.

'Angelo, you wouldn't do anything if he . . . ?'

'I shouldn't do anything I was sorry for,' said Angelo. He was back in the organ seat, swinging his legs. 'We've got a grand business, Minn Lee. Why, we turn over millions of dollars, but there's too much skirt in it. When a dame starts telling a guy to get a guy, and he falls—that's bad.'

'But you like Tony?' said Minn Lee.

Angelo smiled angelically.

179

'Sure. He's a swell feller. But he's got all wrong with Kelly, and he ain't got enough in with the politicians to hold him off. Kelly ain't so hard to get on with either.'

It was one of the few times he had ever spoken to her so freely.

'You must trust me a lot to tell me this,' she said. 'If Tony knew how you felt . . .'

Again that quick, flashing smile of his.

'He'd be dead before he could pull a rod.'

She shook her head helplessly.

'I don't understand you all,' she said, and Angelo explained.

'It's business, ain't it, Minn Lee? These big storekeepers don't allow no competition, do they? And they don't allow bums holding down big jobs. They bounce 'em—we bump 'em. What they do with money we do with rods.'

Tony came in, mopping his brow, and Angelo regarded him critically.

'Mother and child doing fine?' he asked.

Perelli turned with a snarl.

'That's too fresh for me.'

Had he been in anything but this emotional storm he too would have detected a very considerable change in the attitude of his lieutenant.

'You're a swell feller, but there's a place for everybody in this outfit.'

He drank the remainder of the wine that Maria had left, and wiped his streaming face.

'What will she do?' asked Minn Lee.

'She'll stay here,' he said shortly.

'Hasn't she any friends?'

'Yes—me,' he snapped. 'She stays here.'

Angelo was in the way, and Tony turned to him.

'I want to talk to Minn Lee. And, Angelo, I want Minn Lee's car in front'—he looked at his watch—'at six.'

He was sensitive, now that his agitation had worn off, to Angelo's attitude, and, when he had gone:

'He is too fresh, that feller,' he said. 'Grow our own flowers, eh? One of these days . . .'

He had a task to perform and, for a man of sensibility,

180

it was by no means a pleasant task. He sat cross-legged on the broad settee and beckoned her.

'Come here, little Minn Lee. I've just remembered something.'

He took her hand and ran the tips of his fingers up the jewelled arm.

'Swell stuff that, Minn Lee.'

She nodded. She knew exactly what he was going to say, exactly what would happen.

'It's good stuff,' he went on slowly, 'but it ain't up to the minute. All those jewels must be reset for you, Minn Lee. I know a boy at Tiffany's who'll do it swell. You give them to me; I'll have it done right now.'

There was no argument. Very slowly, but without any of the reluctance he expected, she stripped the jewels one by one and dropped them on the settee.

'These will look fine when they're reset,' he went on. 'You'll get them back, Minn Lee, don't you worry. I'll make these sparklers look like a million dollars—while you're away.'

There was emphasis in the last words, and she looked at him.

'While I'm away?' she repeated.

He slipped the jewellery into his pocket.

'Yes, for a little time. This has upset me, but mostly what you told me about Jimmy. I love you too much,' he said dismally. 'When you come back, I will forget.'

There was a long silence. Minn Lee looked at her bare arm with that inscrutable little smile of hers.

'Where am I going?' she asked softly.

He took her hands in his.

'I will tell you. You want to help Tony, don't you, my pretty? I've had a lot of trouble at Cicero. These damn' girls have been robbing me. So I fired the girl at the big 'ouse, eh? She was no good.'

He heard the quick catch of her breath, and was prepared for tears, but they did not come.

'You want me to go there and take her place?' She shook her head.

'For a little while,' he pleaded. 'You're a swell manager, Minn Lee; you'd put everything jake for me. You shall

181

have a grand suite—better than the Blackstone. Servants, cars, have your friends . . .'

She shook her head, and the master in him came out.

'Minn Lee, I have been very good to you,' he said sharply.

'Yes.' She spoke so low that he could hardly hear the word.

'Now you will be a darling and so good,' he said. 'It is for Tony.'

He said this with an air of finality and, cramming the jewels in his pocket, he got up to his feet with his brightest smile.

'Now I will play you something.'

He put his arm about her and they walked slowly to the organ, but she slipped away.

'Play, Tony. I want to write to my dressmaker,' she said.

'Sure.' He sat at the organ and talked throughout the soft aria he was playing. 'I will pay all the accounts,' he said. 'Put them on the table for Angelo. I'll come down and see you, Minn Lee, every day maybe.'

She did not hear him. She had drawn a sheet of notepaper from the rack and was writing quickly. His mind went back to Angelo.

' "Grow our own flowers," eh? That fellow's getting too fresh, Minn Lee. Do you know what he said to me yesterday? He said: "You can dish it out, Tony, but I wonder if you can take it?" To me, Tony Perelli! Was that saying I was yellow . . . gee!'

He felt a hand on his shoulder and looked up into her white face.

'You're not ill?' he said, in consternation.

Her illness at this moment would be extraordinarily complicating.

'No, no, I am not ill.'

'You're a swell girl, Minn Lee.' He patted her hand. 'But you look so white.'

'I've got a headache,' she said.

'Lie down.' He made this concession.

Out of the corner of his eye he saw her drop on to the broad couch and turned his attention again to the organ.

'Angelo, eh? He's too big . . . that's the trouble with all these little shots. You give them somep'n' and they take much. You hear, Minn Lee? . . . Minn Lee, you gone asleep? The car will be here at six.'

He stopped playing, rose and stretched himself. Then he saw the letter she had put on a ledge by the side of the organ. He picked it up, read it carelessly, and then spun round, his face grey with horror.

'Minn Lee! Minn Lee!' he quavered huskily.

She lay very, very still; blood was dripping from the sofa; there was already a big pool on his precious carpet.

'Minn Lee, you damn' fool! You damn' fool!' he shrieked. 'Minn Lee!'

He heard Kelly's voice outside and shrieked his name. The detective came in, took everything in at a glance: the salon, the dead girl lying serene and calm, the horror-stricken gangster.

'What the . . . ? God Almighty!'

He saw the knife in Perelli's hand, the knife he had picked up from the floor.

'Drop it.'

The knife dropped.

'Don't move.'

Perelli was covered with a gun.

'No, no, I didn't do it!' Perelli was gibbering. 'I didn't . . . suicide—there's the letter. Look—the letter! There—she wrote it . . .'

Kelly picked up the letter and read it slowly.

Good-bye, Tony. This is better than Cicero. God bless you!

It bore Minn Lee's signature. He looked at the letter and at Perelli; then, striking a match, he burnt the letter.

'Twenty men you've killed and got away with it,' he said, his voice quivering with hate; 'and now you're going to croak for something you never did—Jesus, that's funny!'

The words came like a douche of cold water to the half-maddened gangster. He sprang to the telephone, gave a number and, as he gave it, Kelly's heart sank. It was the number of a lawyer, one of the greatest of the lawyers. There was no chance. What had seemed an obvious end to Perelli's adventure was not to be an end at all.

183

Kelly watched him, looked down at the ashes of the letter and smiled, looked back at the dead girl and smiled. It was Perelli's trick. There would be an arrest, a trial, the inevitable acquittal for lack of evidence, and that would be that. What was the use? Gangland had established its punishments and its immunities.

He heard the quick, staccato rattle of Perelli's words and walked to the door. He did not see Angelo enter or the quick glance he gave at the dead girl and his instant withdrawal. Behind the door the little Italian stood, his face tense, looking at the woman he loved and from her to the man he hated.

'That is it, Chief.' Perelli's voice was exultant. 'We are the law. You see, you are clever, but not so clever as Tony Perelli. I have told my lawyer exactly what has happened at this moment. . . .'

Angelo opened the door a little wider, felt for the key . . . that was working. He slipped a gun from his pocket and thumbed back the hammer.

'So you see, Mr. Kelly . . .' Tony began again.

Twice Angelo fired through the half-open door and, slamming, locked it, before he fled to the third elevator and freedom.

Kelly spun round at the sound of the shot. Harrigan in the doorway had seen the flash of the revolver and flung across the room. Kelly looked down at the sprawling figure at his feet.

'The law got you, Perelli. Not my law, but your own law. And that's the way of it.'

On the following pages are some details of some Arrow titles that will be of interest.

ROOM 13
by Edgar Wallace

When the gates of Dartmoor closed behind Johnny Gray his cold blue eyes held a menace that was to shock friend and enemy alike. Johnny had a debt to pay the Big Printer, the master forger who had shopped him.

Then there was another problem, for the girl he loved had married the handsome and honest Major Floyd. Johnny was prepared to let the better man win — until he recognised Marney's new husband .....

BIG FOOT
by Edgar Wallace

Superintendent Minter — known as Sooper — believed in hard facts. (Theorising he left to amateur detectives like Gordon Cardew.)

But even Cardew confessed himself baffled by his dour housekeeper, a woman whose secret knowledge led to her strange death in a lonely beach cottage. Cardew could not explain the giant footprints near the locked room in which her body lay. Then Big Foot struck again, and Sooper had another gory mystery to unravel before the solution came from the past and Big Foot was identified.

THE AVENGER
by Edgar Wallace

Mike Brixan, Foreign Office investigator, accepts with some misgivings the task of catching the unknown terror who calls himself the Head-Hunter and who persistently baffles the police with his cold-blooded murders.

When the latest severed head is found, Brixan moves fast. His only clue comes from a beautiful film extra who is a distraction from the business in hand. Grimly Brixan follows the murderer's trail, revealing the workings of a mind twisted by a dark urge for vengeance ...

THE TWISTER
by Edgar Wallace

Immaculate, suave, known in the City as a shrewd financier, and known also as a great expert on the Turf, yet behind the almost languid facade, a hint of ruthlessness and determination. Qualities that a few men had been exposed to.

These were the men who knew him as 'the Twister'. Men who had prided themselves on their financial deviousness and who had met their match.

FLAT 2
by Edgar Wallace

'If that is a threat, it makes me laugh. I am Emil Louba.
I go my way, trampling or stepping over whatever is in
my path. It is for others to choose whether I trample or
step over. But I do not turn aside'.

A philosophy that makes enemies. Many enemies.

But when Louba tried to ensnare Jane Martin, he put
his life in real danger. Danger that led to the final horror
in Flat 2.

THE MIXER
by Edgar Wallace

'Now I'll tell you something', said the girl, and the touch of pink in her cheeks was the only evidence of her emotion. 'There is in London a crook who is going about swindling the swindlers. He is known as The Mixer! I dare say you've heard of him.'

The underworld was becoming painfully aware of a man they called 'The Mixer'. He chose as his victims successful criminals who had enriched themselves at the expense of honest men. An elegant and ruthless operator, the Mixer robbed the swindler, confidence trickster and blackmailer alike.

In all his dealings with these villains, the Mixer was invariably one step ahead.

NO MORE DYING THEN
by Ruth Rendell

The house: an empty, stately shell. The garden, once formal, landscaped, now a neglected wilderness. The statues, sundials, fountains, crumbling, bramble-choked. A jungle of weeds.

Chief Inspector Wexford, born and brought up in that part of the Sussex countryside, remembered playing in the grounds as a child.

Now there was another child. Dead. Described in the official report as 'female, aged about twelve, so far un-identified'. Yet Wexford knew already who she was. Knew also that another child was missing.